The Guardian Mist

# The Guardian Mist

by

Susan Stoker

# Table of Contents

# The Lore of the Lucius Ring

## By Katherine Le Veque

*128 A.D.*
*The Junii Villa, 8 miles northwest of Rome*

IT WAS A strong breeze that swept of the Tyrrenhian Sea, a breeze that was a breath from the gods, from Poseidon as he bellowed angrily at the land which he could not dominate. This summer season had been unusually warm and the sea breezes reflected that unnatural heat. The locals said that it was because Hades had left the gates of hell open and what they were experiencing was the great belches of infernal fire, but Theodosia dismissed the native dramatics as she usually did. Moreover, she had no time for such things. These days, she had little time for anything other than her own grief.

On the placid morning, Theodosia sat upon a cushioned chair in the *peristylium*, a garden area that was towards the rear of her parents' villa outside of Rome. It was a villa that had been in her family for generations, as her family, the Junii, were long-established nobility among the patrician society of Rome. Along with respect and wealth came privilege, and Theodosia's entire life had been one of advantage and pleasure, and when it came time for her to marry, her father (much the slave to his daughter's wishes), allowed her to select her own husband. Select she did, a young and dashing Roman officer from a good family named Lucius Maximus Aentillius.

*Lucius.*

The mere name entering her mind used to bring torrents of tears, ever since the letter from the governor of Londinium, addressed to her father, had been received those six months ago. *It is my sincerest regret to inform you that the Twentieth Victorious Valerian Legion was discovered to be overrun upon the great Vallum Aelium. All within the legion were lost.*

*Lost....*

Now, Theodosia pretended to be numb to the mention of her husband's name because her constant tears frightened her young daughter. *Lucius' daughter.* Whenever she looked into that little face, she saw her husband within in the depths; dark and curly hair, hazel eyes... all of this was Lucius. Mostly, she cried for the child that would never know her father and for the father who never knew he had a child. These days, Theodosia cried many tears for many reasons.

She also cried for herself.

Twenty-three years of age was quite early to be widowed, but that was the position she found herself in. Her family, as well-connected as they were, and with her father being a senator, she knew she would not be able to remain a widow much longer. Already, her father's friend, Proculus Tarquinius Geganius, was filling her father's ear with a stew of poisonous suggestions that would see his son, Marcus, married to Theodosia. Marcus didn't like girl-children, however, so Theodosia's young daughter, Lucia, would have to remain with her grandparents. In spite of the girl-child, however, Marcus was willing to marry the beautiful Theodosia.

Theodosia, however, was unwilling to marry him. Her life, void of joy and cast into a sea of turmoil those six months ago, was threatening to become worse with the axe of marriage hanging over her head. Despair and sorrow were her constant companions. If her parents had anything to say about it, she would marry Marcus and little Lucia would no longer be welcome to live with her mother, but Theodosia would not let that happen.

Above all else, she and Lucia would remain together.

On this warm morning, Theodosia watched Lucia play in the pond in the middle of the *peristylium*, her thoughts lingering on the day she and Lucius had met.

It had happened along the sea shore where she had been walking along with friends and collecting lovely shells. Lucius and some of his cohorts had rowed onto the sand from a Roman warship that had been anchored off shore, invading their shell-gathering, but no one seemed to mind at that point. Theodosia and her friends had been laughing, enjoying life and enjoying the sun, when six brawny soldiers disembarked from their cog.

It was a moment that changed Theodosia's life forever.

The soldiers were quite interested in the women along the beach, but Theodosia's friends fled, leaving Theodosia standing on the beach with her apron full of sea shells. Realizing she was alone, she had tried to flee but the sea shells had fallen to the sand and the next she realized, Lucius was helping her pick them all up. She gazed into the man's gentle, warm eyes and she was lost.

A brief courtship followed in the usual fashion except she discovered her lover to be quite prolific with prose – Lucius would write her poetry, in secret of course, because if his cohorts in the legion caught wind of the fact that Lucius would write songs of love and beauty, he might have been laughed at. But, oh, the prose! The beauty of his words! And the last line, in anything he wrote her, was always the same:

*Cum cogitationes solum de uobis.* With dreams only of you.

Words that had such great meaning to them, in fact, that Lucius had them inscribed on the wedding ring he gave her. It was a family ring that had come through Lucius' very wealthy mother whose family had descended from the Greek gods centuries before. It was said that Silvia's family was half-divine, descended from Mars, and when Lucius gave Theodosia his mother's family ring, he told her that the ring had come from Aphrodite herself. The ring, a very dark gold with a crimson-colored ruby, appeared old enough to have perhaps truly been forged by the gods.

But it was a beautiful ring of great sentimental value. With her parents' permission, Theodosia and Lucius had been married a scant six weeks later and at the reception following their wedding, Lucius' mother, the elegant Lady Silvia, had pulled Theodosia aside. Although the woman had been gracious and affectionate, her attention was not on Theodosia – it had been on the ring.

*As I have no daughters, I asked my son to give you this ring meant from my family,* she had said. *As you wear it upon your finger, I must tell you the legend behind it. Now the ring is a part of you and you are a part of it, and you must pass it down to your daughter, and your daughter must pass it to her daughter. It has been in my family for centuries; some say it was worn by Aphrodite herself. The ring possesses the greatest power of love and when the owner of the ring knows true love, the stone will turn crimson. But if owner of the ring fails to find true love before she has seen twenty-five summers, the stone will turn to dark ember and the owner shall be alone for eternity.*

Theodosia had looked at the ring and it was indeed a lovely crimson color. Puzzled, she had spoken freely. *The stone is crimson upon my finger,* she had said, *but I fear you have gifted me with a generous burden. I fear to tell any daughter I may have that if she does not know love by her twenty-fifth summer, then she shall be an old maid.*

Silvia had laughed. *You needn't worry,* she had said. *Any daughter you and my son will have will surely be beautiful and know love.*

Theodosia still wasn't convinced. *Have you ever seen it actually turn to ember?*

Silvia lost some of her humor. *Once,* she had said, *on my spinster aunt. The stone was black and she died old and alone. But before she died, she gave it to me and I soon wed Lucius' father. The stone turned crimson and has been crimson ever since.*

Even now, in the sunshine of her parent's *peristylium*, Theodosia recalled that conversation and looked at the ring upon her slender finger, which had turned darker shades since the missive from Londinium those months ago. It wasn't exactly a dark ember color, but it was no longer the rich, red crimson it used to be. Odd how she hadn't noticed that before. The ring, before her eyes, was darkening.

Curious as to the changing color of the ring, Theodosia thought on her age; *I have seen twenty-three summers.* Only two more years to find love again or the ring would darken for the rest of her lifetime. What if what Lady Silvia said was true? What if she would never love again if she did not find it in the next two years?

But her thoughts quickly settled; she had loved once before. She and Lucius had shared a love that mortal men could only dream of. She didn't want to find love again; she wanted to remember Lucius forever as her one and only true love. She didn't want another man's touch to erase that memory.

If the ring turned to black, so be it.

"A beautiful morning, my glory."

Theodosia was rocked from her thoughts of the ring by her father, who came up behind her and kissed her on the head. She covered the ring on her finger, putting her hand over it, as she forced a smile at her father.

"Good morn to you as well," she said politely. "Where is mother?"

Tiberius Junius Brutus threw a thumb back in the direction of the *cucina*, or kitchen. "There is some crisis regarding a roasting pig, I think," he said, pulling up a chair. "The truth is that I do not know. I try not to involve myself in your mother's affairs because she will pinch me."

Theodosia giggled. "Pinch her in return."

Tiberius shook his head. "Then she will strike me," he said with fear, watching his daughter laugh. "Nay, daughter; I will remain happily out of your mother's affairs. I have come to see you and Lucia this morning."

Theodosia looked over at her daughter, now picking some of her mother's precious pink flowers.

"Lucia!" she called. "Do not pick those flowers!"

The little girl looked up at her mother, grinned, and moved on to the next bush to pick those flowers. Theodosia sighed.

"She is so much like her father," she said softly. "She knows that her smile will ease everything with me. I cannot become angry when she smiles."

Tiberius laughed softly. "Nor can I," he said, tapping his daughter affectionately on the arm. "When you were young, it was the same way with you. I could deny you nothing when you smiled at me."

Theodosia looked at her beloved father, smiling at the man. "Does it still work?"

He grunted and looked away, aware of her attempt at manipulation. "More than likely."

She chuckled, turning her attention back to her daughter. "That is good to know."

Tiberius cleared his throat again, eyeing his grand-daughter as she ripped yellow posies off the vine before returning his gaze to his daughter. His focus lingered on her, his titian-haired daughter that he loved so much. Her heartbreak had been his heartbreak but, as a father, he had the ability to see the bigger picture in her life. He knew she was still grieving for Lucius but to allow her to wallow in that anguish forever would not be a good thing. Theodosia deserved better things in life that to weep over a lost love.

"You seem happier these days, Theo," he ventured. "You are at least smiling again."

Theodosia knew what he meant and the familiar pangs of grief began to come over her again. "Sometimes," she said. "It comes and goes."

Tiberius continued to watch her, noting the expressions of pain upon her face. "It does not have to be like this forever," he said softly. "The time will come again when you are happy. Sometimes the best thing to do is to find another source of happiness."

Theodosia rolled her eyes and stood up. "I do not want to find another source of happiness, Father," she said firmly. "If you are going to bring up Proculus and his pompous son, do not bother. I will not marry Marcus. He means to separate me from my child and I will not have it. It is barbaric."

Tiberius remained calm as his daughter's ire rose. "He is a man who has never been married," he said evenly. "He does not understand the attachment between a mother and her child. I am sure that in time he will come to understand it. He is not an unreasonable man; in fact, he has a very bright future ahead of him. Some say he is to be the next proconsul of Byzantium. He is in much favor with Caesar. You could be his wife, Theodosia, and command much wealth and power. Does this not appeal to you?"

Theodosia was looking at her political-savvy father in horror; she knew the man saw her match to Marcus as a great political marriage that would bring both families prestige. But she wanted no part of it.

"And I must sacrifice my child in order to attain it?" she asked, aghast. Then, she shook her head firmly. "Nay, Father; I will not sacrifice Lucia simply to gain a new husband. I do not *want* a new husband. I thought you understood this."

Tiberius understood it all too well, but he also understand that he, as Theodosia's father, knew what was best for her. He and his wife had been given over to many long discussions about their daughter's future and Theodosia's mother was also in agreement. They had to do what was best for their child, whether or not she realized it. Lucius was dead and he was never coming back. Theodosia, with or without Lucia, had to move on. But the difficulty would be in the doing.

"Theo," Tiberius said quietly as he rose from his chair. Theodosia was facing the small fish pond in the *peristylium,* refusing to look at him. When he realized she wasn't going to turn around to face him, he cleared his throat softly. "I understand that you are still grieving for Lucius. I understand that you loved the man. But you must understand that life goes on without him. Lucius is dead, Theo; he has been dead for years as far as we know. You have therefore been a widow for at least that long. Will you waste your life lingering in the past, over a love that grew cold years ago? You are more intelligent than that. You were always given free choice in all matters but I find that at this time, I must make your decisions for you since you choose to linger in the darkness. I told Marcus that you would marry him. The contract has been sealed. Tomorrow, Marcus will come for you and you will go with him. You must trust me in this matter, Theodosia. I know what is best for you."

Theodosia had been staring at the fish pond through his speech until he mentioned Marcus and the marriage. Realizing what her father had done, she looked at the man in outrage.

"You had no right!" she hissed. "No right at all!"

Tiberius would not be sucked into her argument. He turned away. "As your father and the man who provides your food and clothing, I have every right," he told her sternly. "I am sorry if this angers you, Theo, but you will thank me one day. This is what is best for you. Lucia will remain here with your mother and I until such time as Marcus will allow her into his household.

She will be happy here, I swear it."

Tiberius was walking away, as he often did with face with enraged or emotional females. Theodosia knew it would do no good to scream at him for it would only make him angry. It would only drive him away to the point where he would lock himself in his room and refuse to come out. Nay, arguing with the man would not bring about his change of mind. Once his mind was set, it was purely stone.

Tears filling her eyes, Theodosia watched her father disappear into the villa, no doubt to inform Theodosia's mother what he had done. *She probably already knows*, Theodosia thought bitterly. She was quite certain they had both had a hand in this because she was also quite certain that her father had tried to deliver this news to her more than once over the past few days but she was in no frame of mind to listen to him. But today, he could no longer delay, especially if Marcus was expecting her on the morrow. Was it really possible?

*Oh, God… Marcus…!*

Theodosia could not go to him; she *would* not go to him. She would not leave her daughter behind. That being the case, she would either have to fight the man off or run away from him. She chose to run; there was nothing left for her here, anyway, not with Lucius gone. In fact, this entire place reminded her of him, reminded her of the man she had loved and lost. She had to go somewhere else and start anew, a place where there were no memories of Lucius and where overbearing buffoons like Marcus weren't breathing down her neck.

She had to get away.

Lucia was still picking yellow flowers off the vine as her mother came to her and gently led her away. Into the dark, well-furnished villa they went, heading to the *cubiculum* they shared, the one that Theodosia had shared with Lucius before he'd left for Britannica. The chamber was small but well-appointed with a comfortable larger bed and then a smaller one in the corner for Lucia.

Once inside the chamber, Theodosia shut the door and bolted it. The only light and air came from a narrow window up near the ceiling, a window that faced inward to the atrium of the home. On the second floor of the villa as they were, the walls of the chamber were painted beautiful reds and yellows, with a woodland scene against the outer wall.

Lucius had once taken a reed brush and, with black paint he'd taken from the household slaves that worked the maintenance on the villa, painted a giant penis on every animal in the woodland scene. The enormous phalluses were still there and gave Theodosia cause to smile every time she saw them. They reminded her of Lucius and his sense of humor, of the man who could be so loving and yet so naughty at times. She loved that about him. They risqué paintings brought a smile to her lips even now.

So she stood there a moment, grinning at her husband's sense of humor, drinking in the sight to tuck back into her memory for days when she was feeling particularly lonely. She could lose herself in thoughts of Lucius so easily here but she eventually shook them off. She had a job to do. Opening the large chest where clothes and other possessions were kept, she removed a large satchel made from leather and fabric. Quickly, she went to work.

As Theodosia hurriedly packed, Lucia found her poppets and sat upon her little bed, paying with her dolls and the flowers she had picked. At one point, Theodosia's mother knocked on her door, wanting to speak with her, but Theodosia chased her away. She didn't want to speak with her mother. She knew the woman supported her husband's decision to marry off their daughter so she had no desire to speak with her. She had no desire to speak with the woman who would so greedily accept Lucia to raise as her own.

So Theodosia's mother eventually wandered away, distraught, but Theodosia didn't pay the woman any mind. She continued packing her bag, stuffing it with clothing they would need and valuables to sell, including every piece of jewelry her father had ever given her. They were expensive pieces and would bring a goodly sum. Theodosia knew she would need the money.

As she bustled about in her chamber, collecting things of value, she passed by her writing desk and accidentally bumped into it. Pieces of vellum fell to the floor and as she picked them up, her attention was focused on one particular sheet on the top.

*My fingers brush the sky; I see your face in the clouds.*
*In white mist, your smile fills my soul,*
*My heart has wings!*
*Upon the breath from the sea, I hear you call to me,*
*Ever, Theodosia, ever my love!*
*For separation cannot deny the bonds of our passionate hearts.*

With a sigh, Theodosia slowed in her packing as she read the poem, twice. Lucius had been known to write copious amounts of poetry to her and she, in turn, had learned to write it to him. But that had stopped the moment the missive had come from Londinium. She never wanted to write poetry ever again, for it was something only meant for Lucius. Looking at her words upon the vellum, words she'd hoped to give to Lucius someday, she missed the man all the more. It made her realize that running away was the right thing to do. She would not be separated from the child of the man who instilled such love within her breast. For him, still, her heart had wings and it always would.

She renewed her packing with a sense of urgency

now, stronger than before. Her next order of business was to dress her daughter appropriately for travel and she bundled the child up in loosely fitting clothing. Putting a little cap on her head to conceal her dark curls, she dressed appropriately herself in durable traveling clothing. Her dark red hair, so shiny and lovely, was wrapped up in a scarf to conceal it. Dressed and packed, she fed her child the remnants of the fruit and bread and cheese that had been left over from a mid-morning meal and waited for the sun to set.

There was a reason she wanted to wait until sundown; she knew her parents would be taking their naps before the evening meal and the villa would be quiet and still for the most part. Opening her chamber door as the sunlight on the walls turned shades of pink and gold, she slipped from her chamber and down the stairs that led to the *vestibulum*, or entry, as her chamber was very close to it.

There were a few servants about but they didn't notice her as she slipped out into the olive grove that was immediately outside, using the darkened trees with their dark green leaves so shield her flight. As the night birds began to forage overhead and the sea breeze blew cool and damp, Theodosia and Lucia slipped away from *Villa Junii,* making their way to the inland road that would lead to the north.

It was a long flight into the night that did not stop

even when the sun rose again. It was well into the next day when Theodosia, carrying the sleeping Lucia on her shoulder as she trudged down the tree-lined road, heard the sounds of a wagon behind her. Fearful it might be her father, for she had already evaded his patrols twice, she slipped off the road and allowed the cart to pass, noting it was a lone man with an empty cart. The wagon bed was covered in chaff.

Hopeful that she might have found a ride to the mountainous interior region where she hoped to find shelter, she came out of her hiding place and began to walk quickly after the cart. She could only pray the man at the reins was a kind and moral soul. At this point she didn't much care because her exhaustion and hunger had the better of her. She needed rest and food badly, overriding her common sense.

"Sir?" she called after him. "*Sir?*"

The man in the cart, hearing the voice behind him, turned around to the source but kept going. However, when he saw the woman with the small child following him, he came to a halt. Relieved, Theodosia ran up to the wagon bench.

"Good sir," she said, weary and hopeful. "Would you be kind enough to take my child and I with you?"

The man, younger, with handsome and somewhat rugged blond looks, nodded. "Where are you going?"

Theodosia lifted the half-asleep Lucia onto the wagon bench and the man grasped the child so she wouldn't slither away. Theodosia climbed up onto the bench and took Lucia back into her arms, holding the child tightly.

"I... I am going up this road a way," she said, uncertain what to tell the man who seemed to be gazing at her with some interest. "Thank you for your graciousness."

The man clucked softly at the big brown horse, who began to walk again. He eyed Theodosia somewhat, curious about the beautiful woman with the sleeping child. He also noticed the traveling clothes, the bag. "Have you been traveling far?" he asked politely.

Theodosia nodded. "Very far."

"Where are you going?"

Theodosia had no idea what to tell him so she avoided answering. She glanced at the wagon bed, covered in chaff. "Are you a farmer?" she asked.

The man nodded. "My father and I have a large farm near Cesaro," he said. "I go into Rome once a week to sell our produce at the markets. I am just returning."

Theodosia glanced at the man; he had pale blue eyes and very big, muscular hands. "What do you sell?"

"Grain, mostly," he said. "We also have a small vineyard and my father makes wine."

Theodosia was interested in such a life; men and women who worked the land had always fascinated her. *To be so useful,* she thought. She had no idea what it truly meant to be useful, just as she had no idea what it truly meant to run away from her father's home. Already, they had faced some hunger and hardship. She was frightened. But she also felt strangely free.

"Do you do well at the market?" she asked, genuinely curious. "That is to say, are you able to do well enough to feed yourself and your family?"

When he caught her looking at him, he smiled and his eyes crinkled. "I do well enough," he told her. "But it is just my father and me. There are only two mouths to feed."

"No wife?"

"I was married, once, but she died giving birth to my son, who also died."

Theodosia sobered. "I am sorry," she said. "I did not mean to pry."

The man shook his head. "You did not," he said, eyeing her now with more interest than curiosity. "My name is Gaius, by the way."

"I am Theodosia. This is my daughter, Lucia."

"Where are you going, Theodosia? To see your family?"

Theodosia shook her head and looked away. "Nay."

"Your husband, perhaps?"

Again, she shook her head. "My husband is dead."

"And you are running from his cruel family who beats you daily and forces you into slavery?"

Theodosia grinned in spite of her herself. "Nay," she

said. "I have been living with my family. My husband's family is all dead."

Gaius was an extraordinarily intelligent man for being a farmer; in fact he had been schooled in his youth and spent several years in the Roman army, but an ill father and a failing farm had caused him to return home.

Bright as he was, he knew there was much more to Theodosia than she was telling him. She was a stunningly beautiful woman with soft white hands and smooth skin and if he could guess about her, he would say she was a noblewoman. She just had that look about her, regal and elegant. But she was running from something, or someone, and the protective male in him seemed to be taking great interest in her. It probably wasn't healthy for him, for he'd never had good fortune with women, but he couldn't help himself. Something about Theodosia drew him to her.

But she obviously didn't feel the same way about him. She had refused to answer his questions about where she was going so he was coming to suspect that perhaps she didn't even know. She appeared very tired and hungry, and her little girl was exhausted. He was more than likely a fool for being sympathetic to her, but he was.

"If your destination is too far away, my farm is only an hour ahead," he told her casually. "It is getting late. If you would like to rest the night, as our guest, we would be happy to have you and your daughter. In fact, my dog just had a litter of puppies your daughter might like to play with. Otherwise, they will be very lonely puppies."

Theodosia looked at the man, shocked by his offer. *Do not agree!* She told herself, suspicious of the Gaius' ulterior motive. But the truth was that a night in a safe home with a warm fire was too good to resist. Perhaps it would be the most foolish thing she ever did in her life to accept his invitation, but she found herself quite willing to do it. For her daughter's sake, she had to.

"Well," she said, pretending to be reluctant. "I suppose we could, just for the night, of course. We would be gone by sunrise."

Gaius nodded. "As you wish," he said, eyeing her. "If… if you perhaps need to earn some money for your trip, there are chores about the farm that need to be done. I would pay you for them."

Theodosia looked at him in surprise. "Chores?" she repeated, both disgusted and intrigued. "Like what?"

Gaius grinned at the dismay in her tone, which only proved his theory that she was a noblewoman who did not do manual work. "Milking the goats," he told her. "Sweeping. Cooking. We can always use help if you are looking for a job."

*A job.* Theodosia had to admit that she was very interested. It would be some place for her and Lucia to stay, to be together, and for her to earn a living even though she'd never earned a living in her life. Still, it might be the opportunity she needed. She tried not to seem too eager about it.

"We can discuss it, I suppose," she said. "But you should know I have never milked a goat in my life."

He grinned, glancing at her lily-white hands. "Is that so?" he said, somewhat wryly. "I would never have guessed. It is easy to learn."

"Is it?"

"I can will teach you."

"I cannot cook, either."

"I can teach you that, too."

Theodosia thought, perhaps, that it all sounded too good to be true. Were the gods sending her a sign or was Hades providing a trap for being a disobedient daughter? She couldn't be sure, but she was attracted to Gaius' offer. It was a struggle not to become excited about it.

"But my daughter must stay with me," she said. "You do not mind a child about?"

Gaius shook his head. "My father always wanted a grandchild. He will like having her about."

Theodosia didn't know what to say; she was coming to think that, indeed, the gods knew of her plight and had brought Gaius into her life at precisely the correct time. Was it even possible that all of this could be true?

She would soon find out.

Gaius and his father, Agrippus, lived like two bachelors on a very large farm. There was plenty of work to be done and Theodosia wasn't afraid to learn. In fact, she rather liked it. Gaius taught her to cook and to milk goats, to press wine and make flour. Theodosia learned quickly. She soon came to love her new life and, in time, love for Gaius bloomed as well. A truly good-hearted man who readily accepted Lucia, Theodosia knew that the decision to leave her parents' home had been the best decision she had ever made. She knew that Lucius would have approved.

With the introduction of Gaius, the ring that Lucius had given her those years ago once again turned a deep, rich crimson and would remain so until the day Theodosia passed it on to Lucia on the day of her eighteenth birthday. Fortunately for Lucia, the ring would turn crimson two years later at the introduction of a certain young soldier who happened to cross her path.

The ring of Lucius' family, the ring of true love or of lost love, continued to live on through the ages, passed down from Lucia to her daughter, and from her daughter onward. The story of the ring was also passed along with it, an oral tradition for the female members of the family, and through the centuries, the eldest daughter of each generation would hold great hope that the ring would turn crimson for her. Somewhere along the line, it was said that if one spoke the words inscribed upon the ring, *with dreams only of you*, that a lover would appear within a fortnight. Many a young woman believed in those words. Many a young woman was rewarded for that belief.

But a few were not. No one could be sure why those spellbound words sometimes worked or sometimes didn't, or why love would turn the stone to crimson and heartache would turn it to black, but it didn't really matter. It was a glorious tradition within the females of the family and the mystery of the crimson-stoned ring continued to brand Theodosia's descendants with its particular kind of magic.

The lore of the Lucius Ring lived on.

*Prologue*

*Twenty-Four Years Ago*

"PUSH, CASSIA, PUSH. These babies aren't going to be born by themselves."

Cassia Velt bit back a curse and clenched her teeth. If her mom didn't shut up, she was gonna kill her. It wasn't as if she hadn't given birth before. She had...five years ago. But unfortunately, it seemed that the curse that hung over their family wasn't broken. She had one more shot at getting rid of it once and for all.

The curse of the family ring that had been handed down from mother to daughter for as long as anyone could remember was on Cassia's mind almost every day of her life. The poesy ring was nothing special to look at. Dark gold with a gray-colored stone that legend says might be some sort of really dark ruby. But her mom had tried to polish it more than once and it never looked anything but gray. A dark, disturbing color that made it hard to look at.

1

The legend of the ring maintained it should be passed down from mother to eldest daughter. The stone would turn a brilliant crimson when each woman found her true love, but it had to happen before she turned a quarter of a century old. If she didn't, the ring would turn dark and stay that way, making it impossible for the owner to ever find true love in her lifetime.

Cassia grunted as the nurse encouraged her to push just one more time and looked up to her mother.

Juno Velt was an unhappy woman. As was her mother and also *her* mother. Unhappiness ran rampant in their family, as if each generation made it a goal to make the next as miserable as possible.

Cassia had done all she could to find her true love, as the legend foretold, but in the end, had found nothing but bitterness and misery.

She hadn't ever wanted to get pregnant, wanting to end the curse once and for all. Not having a daughter to pass the ring to would certainly do that—but the Roman gods had taken that decision out of her hands.

Despite being religious about birth control with Bobby and making him wear a condom every time they had sex, she'd ended up pregnant anyway, a year after they'd moved in together.

Of course it had been a daughter.

Of course Bobby hadn't wanted anything to do with a baby and had split.

Of course her mom had been pissed.

It was Juno who'd had the not-so-great idea that maybe if they sent the baby away with the ring, it might end the curse for all of them.

That didn't work.

Theodosia's damned ring haunted Cassia's dreams and wouldn't let her rest, even after she'd given away her firstborn. She knew Theodosia and Lucius' story; of course she did. Juno had told her the fairytale so many times when she was little, Cassia could recite it by memory by the time she was four.

Still, for a time, Cassia had managed to push the fact that she'd given away her baby to the back of her head, ignoring the dreams she had each night of swords, Roman soldiers and castles, and going on with her life.

But apparently ancient curses didn't care about rules…because she'd been knocked up again. This time by a one-night stand. With twins. Twin *girls*.

Karma was a bitch.

Cassia wasn't the smartest woman in the world, but when the dreams increased in intensity and she saw the ring in every single one, even *she* knew she was getting a second chance, whether she wanted it or not.

A second chance to help her new eldest daughter find love and free them all from the curse.

"One more push and your first daughter will be here!" the nurse enthused.

Easy for her to say. She wasn't lying on an uncomfortable bed with her legs strapped into stirrups and her cooter on display to any doctor, intern, and orderly who happened to walk into the room.

Cassia pushed thoughts of the ring and the curse out of her mind, and concentrated on the nurse's directions to push.

Ten minutes later, Cassia watched as the nurses wiped, dried, soothed, and sucked icky fluids from the mouths and bodies of her two healthy daughters.

"Make sure you mark the oldest," she told one of the nurses.

"What?"

"Mark the oldest. I have to make sure I know which came first."

"Of course," the nurse said as she weighed one of the newborns. "We'd do that anyway. We'll note it on her bracelet."

Cassia didn't know why, but she felt the need to explain herself to the nurses. "I need to make sure the oldest is differentiable from the younger one. It's a long story, but there's a lot of family history, involving inheritances, and they'll both lose out if we don't know which was first."

"You don't have to explain. It's hospital policy to make note of birth order," the nurse at her feet explained in a brusque tone.

Cassia sighed in relief. It might be hospital policy, but the nurses had no idea how important it was. They were free to find love in their own time and in their own way. This new baby, the oldest, had only twenty-five years, otherwise she was doomed to be alone and miserable forever.

The other nurse smiled at Cassia. "Congratulations, they're both healthy and happy and look amazingly alike, even down to their red hair. You're a very blessed woman."

Cassia heard her mom snort but ignored it, exhausted. Tired of her life, tired of being unhappy, tired of the curse hanging over her head. She wasn't sure exactly how curses worked, but there was obviously an ancient god out there somewhere who was displeased with the trick she'd tried to pull by giving up her firstborn, and was getting back at her.

How did she know?

She'd dreamed it.

A beautiful woman had come to Cassia in a dream.

She'd had weird dreams all her life, but this one was different. It had seemed so *real*. The woman had been wearing a damn toga and sat on some uncomfortable-looking stone bench thing. A man was standing next to her. He was good looking, even if he looked funny in his matching toga with leaves in his dark hair, which was too long and curling around his neck. His hazel eyes were piercing and Cassia somehow knew he could kill a man without a second thought. But when he'd looked down at the woman at his side, his eyes lost that lethal glow and softened.

The woman was tall and slender and had beautiful dark auburn hair, unlike Cassia's own pale red frizzy mop that she'd loathed her entire life. In the dream, the woman had reached up and taken the man's hand, and Cassia saw the reason her life was miserable on the woman's finger. The ring. It shone crimson, so bright that it made Cassia's heart hurt at the sight she'd never gotten a glimpse of in her entire life. Nor had any of the women in the three generations before her.

The woman's voice was soft and melodic and made Cassia want to weep, it was so sad and beautiful at the same time. "You have been given another opportunity to make things right. Your firstborn will find her true love. She will live a long and happy life, as will *her* daughters—but that happiness will not trickle down to you. The ring must be returned to your family and you will be granted another eldest daughter."

Cassia had always been defiant and even in her dreams was no different. "How can I have *another* oldest daughter? That doesn't make sense."

"You are pregnant with a girl. This is another man's child and she is the oldest of *that* man's loins. You have another chance to make this right. For your future, for her future, and the future of your granddaughters twenty times over. It's up to you. This is your absolute last opportunity. The ring has been dark for too long. This is the last chance for you, for the ring, and for your ancestors."

"Damn it all to hell!" Cassia had spat in her dream. "It's not that easy to find true love in this century! Not like it was for you."

"Lucius and I have discussed this. You're right. Times were already very different even one hundred years before you were born. Your ancestors all had difficulties finding their loves, but not like Marcellina, Maxima, and Juno."

Cassia had thought the woman in her dream might be Theodosia, the woman who had started the legend, but referring to the man by her side as Lucius confirmed it. How she knew the names of her great-grandma, grandma, and mother was beyond Cassia, but it was a dream, so she guessed anything was possible.

"Your daughter will experience signs throughout her life, hinting at her soulmate, so when they cross paths, she'll recognize him immediately. The man meant to be hers will also have some unusual experiences and there will be no doubt in *his* mind that she belongs to him. They'll have an instant connection, which will be tested in the worst way. But, heed my words, Cassia, no more trickery. The legend will not be denied."

Cassia had sighed in the dream and said in a sad voice, "I can't go through the rest of my life as miserable as I've been since I turned twenty-five. And I'm afraid to tell my daughter that if *she* doesn't find her true love by the time she's twenty-five, she'll be an old, unhappy spinster like her mother, grandmother and great-grandmother."

Lucius had nodded at her then and said in a deep, soothing voice that seemed to surround her in the large dream chamber she was standing in, "That's the same thing Theodosia said to *my* mother when she gave her the ring."

"And what did your mom say?" Cassia asked, hopefully.

"Any daughter you will have will surely be beautiful and know love."

Cassia had woken up abruptly after that, his words ringing in her ears, and put a hand to her slightly rounded belly. She had another chance to be happy. A daughter who would be beautiful? Sounded good to her.

It was not even a month later Cassia found out she was having twins.

Twin girls.

Damn the gods for having a wicked sense of humor.

Hands at her thighs brought her back to the present with a jolt. Cassia closed her eyes, ignoring the antiseptic smell of the air around her in the hospital, the low murmur of the nurses, even her afterbirth being delivered and her nether region being cleaned up, and, instead, dreamed of a day in the future when her daughter would find a man to love and thus break the curse of her family.

Maybe, just maybe, she herself would finally have a chance to find a man who wouldn't cheat, hit, or otherwise treat her like crap. It wouldn't matter if she was in her sixties when it happened, Cassia would take happiness any way she could get it.

She'd done the obligatory "hold your new daughters and look happy" thing when the nurses had shoved the babies into her arms, but had handed them over to Juno as quickly as she could. She just wasn't cut out to be a mother, but it looked like she had no choice. It wasn't that she didn't want her daughters to be healthy, but her mind was whirling with all that needed to happen in only twenty-five years. It might seem like a lifetime to some, but Cassia knew better. The years would go by way too fast, and along with them, her own chance at happiness and love.

"We'll just take these precious girls to the nursery and get them settled in," the blonde nurse told Cassia and Juno. "The doctor will be in to check you over soon and we'll bring your daughters back later so you can nurse."

"Thank you," Cassia said tiredly.

The blonde nurse nodded and gathered one of the babies into her arms. The dark-haired nurse next to her did the same with the other child.

"She did a good job; she deserves a rest. She can get to know her daughters and fill out the birth certificates afterward," the first nurse said to Cassia's mom.

Juno grunted in response.

The nurses headed out of the room and down the hall to the nursery.

"God, that is one stone-cold bitch," Roberta, the blonde nurse, exclaimed as she soothed a hand over the head of the precious baby in her arms.

"I feel bad for these two. It's obvious there isn't a lot of love in that family. Any sign of the father?" the dark-haired nurse, Susie, asked.

"Nope. I heard the mom harping on her daughter, something about a *curse* and she should've known he wouldn't want more than one night with her, or something."

"God, I hate people sometimes." Susie sighed then looked over at Roberta. "Do you know which of these two angels was first?"

The other nurse laughed uncomfortably. "Crap, no. I was hoping you did. I wasn't watching when mom was holding them and they look exactly alike, so I wasn't sure which was which when they were handed back."

"If anyone finds out we weren't doing our job, we

could get fired. But I'm sure it doesn't really matter. Just pick one and I'll mark it on her armband. No one will ever know the difference," Susie stated decisively. "There's no way I'm going back and telling them I have no idea which was the firstborn. They'd lose it."

"Good idea."

The nurses disappeared into the nursery and got the two newest babies settled in a single crib. They snuggled together, as if they were still in their mother's womb, their arms intertwining and their foreheads resting against each other. They looked exactly the same, weighed exactly the same, and had identical cute pert noses and tufts of red hair on their small heads. The only difference at the moment was a notation on one of the armbands, indicating who was born first.

As the twins took their first nap outside of the warm womb they'd spent the last nine months in, one daughter slept the sleep of the dead, dreamless and devoid of any kind of feeling, good or bad.

The other daughter, the one who had been designated as the younger twin, dreamed of being held close in someone's arms…the smell of something the baby had no intellectual capacity to understand, much less name in her hours-old brain, but something comforting. It came in the form of a mist that covered her and her sister as they slept. She snuggled into the body at her side, feeling safe and wanted.

# Chapter One

V ARINIA VELT'S FINGERS flew over the keyboard in front of her.

She'd found her sister.

Well, half-sister.

Rin had known her entire life that she had a half-sister out there somewhere. From the time she was very young, her mom had told her and Augustina about her. Built her up in their young minds. She was given up for adoption at birth, because of some awful circumstance their mom had never been that clear about. Cassia had told them she'd always regretted giving up her baby and wanted to find her. Was desperate to find her.

Reading the email MacKenzie Reign had sent her had cleared up a lot of things.

A lot.

Like, *a lot* a lot.

Rin had known her entire life that their mom liked

her twin sister, Tina, better than her. In some ways, that was an advantage. After all, when they were young, Rin was allowed to stay up later, could play outside in the dirt, could choose her own friends, and was free to major in whatever she wanted when she got to college. In Rin's mind, Tina had the tougher life. As their mom's favorite, she had to be perfect and was under scrutiny all the time. Her hair had to be flawless. Clothes pressed and clean. No dirt under her nails, friends chosen carefully. She'd attended the nearby private school, while Rin went to public schools.

Still, Rin had grown up in Tina's shadow. It had been hard not to be at least a little bitter growing up. There were even years where Rin had hated her mother. But once she'd made friends in middle and high school, and had realized what her sister had to go through, she'd slowly come to terms with their wildly different lives.

They were twins, but even more different now that they were adults. Oh sure, they were both five feet six inches tall. Both had red hair and curves that women all over the world would kill for. Rin and Tina even had the same freckles that would pop out on their bodies wherever the sun kissed their flesh. But they weren't equals. At least not in Cassia Velt's eyes.

Tina had long, beautiful auburn hair, but their mom had kept Rin's short when they were growing up; a pixie cut that curled around her neck and face, especially when it got just a tad too long. Rin had gotten used to it, and now actually preferred the shorter cut, never bothering to grow it out.

Tina wore beautiful dresses and designer clothes. Rin wore clothes from thrift shops.

Tina had pedicures and manicures. Rin wasn't ever invited to come along.

Tina still got a healthy allowance to do with what she wanted. Rin had gotten her first job at the age of thirteen, bagging food at the local mom-and-pop grocery story, and wasn't given any money from her mom for extras.

Tina had been the most popular girl in her prestigious high school, even elected prom queen her senior year. Rin had been just one of thousands in her class, and while the other members of the computer club thought she was awesome, no one else had even remembered who she was when asked at their five-year reunion.

And all the twins had heard growing up was how sad their mom was for having to give up their sister. When Juno, their grandmother, was alive, she'd told them a story about a woman who'd tragically had to put her baby girl up for adoption. Mom was young, mom was poor, mom was heartbroken at having to give away her beautiful baby daughter, but she wanted the best for her, wanted her to be able to have food on the table every night. And the only way to accomplish that was to give her to a loving family who could provide everything Cassia Velt could not. The only thing she'd left with the baby was a ring that had been in their family forever, so she'd know she was loved by her biological mother.

But the email Rin was reading from MacKenzie gave lie to her mom and grandmother's bullshit.

And it was *all* bullshit.

Rin shouldn't be surprised—she knew her mom, had grown up knowing exactly what her strengths and weaknesses were—but she somehow still was.

She'd used her computer skills and some of her nerdy friends to track down the missing sister. Social media blasts, help from sympathetic county workers who'd dug up ancient paperwork, dogged determination, and some threats from her mother lighting a fire under Rin's butt had finally coughed up the name, MacKenzie O'Neil Reign née Velt, which had led to the surprising fact that the woman now lived in England with her husband...who just happened to be loaded, friends with *the* Prince William, was a viscount, and went by the name of "Lord Reign."

Rin hadn't told her mother yet. She wanted more information on the ring that she'd heard about her entire life before she spilled the beans about the long-lost daughter—and the ring—being found. Both Juno and Cassia had told the twins about the family curse so many times, Rin had it memorized by the time she was three.

If Tina, as the oldest twin, didn't find her one true love by the time she was twenty-five, they'd *all* end up miserable and unhappy the rest of their lives.

Tina had bought into it, and had gotten more and more desperate as the years creeped closer to their magical twenty-fifth birthday. Rin, frankly, couldn't drum up the angst about the legend or the ring that her sister had. She was perfectly happy without a man in her life, thank you very much, and didn't much care about the ring business one way or the other.

As differently as they were raised, it was no wonder she and Tina had such different thoughts about the curse. Men were *meh* in Rin's mind. She'd had boyfriends and male friends, she certainly wasn't a virgin, but because of the way she was raised, in a matriarchal family with a lack of males, she'd learned to do almost everything she needed done by herself. When she'd gone away to college, she'd learned even more about unclogging toilets, resetting circuits, changing tires, and basic plumbing the hard way.

However, D-day was almost here, their twenty-fifth birthday. Thirty-one days and counting, to be exact, before they were cursed for all eternity, yet Rin didn't feel any sense of pressure about their situation.

But Rin *did* feel the want to find her half-sister and

it wasn't just because her mom had become increasingly desperate in the last year. It was probably too late in life for her and the unknown half-sister to ever be close, but this MacKenzie person was someone who had the same blood flowing in her veins.

The second she'd read the email from her half-sister, Rin had known everything was different. The reunion she might've had in her mind—where MacKenzie would be overjoyed to find her mom and the sisters she hadn't known existed—wouldn't ever happen. Her life had spun on its axis and Rin was still reeling from the information MacKenzie had shared.

*Dear Varinia,*

*I have no idea how you found me, but I'm mostly pleased you have. I've thought I was alone my entire life, an orphan, and I am cautiously pleased that I have not only one, but two sisters.*

*With that being said, as much as I once dreamed my mother and father would realize the mistake they made and come back and find me and love me, I've learned what true love is, and have no desire to ever set foot in my birth mother's presence. I'm sorry to be so blunt, you must love her, but it's true.*

*I can only imagine that she told you a fairytale of how she had to give me up and a nice family adopted me. The truth is that I was abandoned* outside a fire station, because she knew they'd have to take me in and do something with me. I was in foster homes until I was six years old and was finally adopted by a wonderful woman named Isobel, who was my mother in every sense of the word.

My husband scoffed at your letter, thinking you were just after our money, or maybe even wanted to meet up with me to get to the Royal Family, but when we read about the description of the ring your mother implored you to find, he relented and agreed that I should write you back.

I do *have the ring. I haven't ever told anyone about it, but Isobel gave it to me when I was eighteen and said it was in the box that I was found in when I was a baby. I can only assume that part of the story your mother told you was true, but for one detail.*

*It is no longer dark, it's a brilliant crimson color, and I believe it's found its true home here in England. It's a long story involving swords and ancient legends, and I truly hope you'll hear it someday, but the truth is stranger than fiction.*

*I'm rambling now, but I still, at that point, wasn't going to email you back, or at the very most was going to tell you that you had the wrong person.*

*But you said you've always had dreams.*

*There is an inscription on the ring that, trans-*

lated from Latin, says: With Dreams Only of You. *Did you know that? Odd dreams are what led me to England and to my husband. I don't know what kind of dreams you're having, or if you're really having them at all, that could be a lie, but if you are, and they are anything like mine were, I imagine you aren't sleeping well.*

*The bottom line is that my husband investigated you and your family. Thoroughly. Enough for him to know you live in a not-so-nice part of Columbus and that you should probably move to a safer place. Enough to know that your mother and sister are living in a nice house on the other side of the city. Enough to know that I think I'd like you a lot more than your twin. Enough to know how desperately your mother and sister are searching for Tina's one true love.*

*The party being planned for your twenty-fifth birthday is Tina's last chance; we both know that. I'm going to do you a favor, because I had a dream about you and that party last night. I've never really understood my dreams, but this one, with dragons, fog and a cityscape, I couldn't even begin to understand.*

*Please know, I'm not doing this out of the goodness of my heart. If it was up to me, I'd never let the ring out of my sight. Ever.*

*But I will send it via courier. On one condi-*

*tion.*

*That* you *wear it. Not your sister. You.*

*You can let your mother and sister know you have it, but it stays on your finger. As soon as the party is over and your sister finds, or doesn't find, her true love, the ring comes back to England. If I understand the legend, it won't matter after that point. The stone in the ring will either be gray or crimson and location won't make a difference. Yes?*

*I'm doing this for you, Varinia. I've never had a sister and I think I just might like you. Maybe after your birthday and whatever's happened has happened, you might take a trip to England.*

*I look forward to hearing your reply.*

*Please let me know if you have any questions,*
*Sincerely, MacKenzie Reign*

Rin had read the email so many times she'd almost memorized it, but couldn't resist glancing at it again. Not only had she finally found her half-sister, but she'd found the ring too.

Cassia couldn't be trusted. Rin knew that, knew her mom was unstable when it came to the family curse and the damn ring. She'd want to keep the ring, or at the very least have Tina wear it, but MacKenzie had demanded that *Rin* wear it, and she knew she'd do whatever her half-sister wanted, just to have a shot at seeing the infamous poesy ring she'd heard about her entire life.

Rin and Tina *were* having a joint birthday party. Rin knew her mom was only holding it as a hail-Mary hope that Tina would find her true love. And Rin was only invited because it would look bad if one of the twins was left out of the celebration. She should've been weirded out that MacKenzie knew about the party, but it wasn't any stranger than family curses. Besides, she couldn't get the line, "I've never had a sister and I think I just might like you" out of her head. She'd love to get to know MacKenzie better and maybe even have the kind of relationship with her that she'd never had with Tina.

In a dream just last night, Rin had walked up to a stranger on the street, and the other woman had said those exact words to her, smiled and walked away.

Right after she'd left, Rin had found herself suddenly in a dark room. It was pitch black and silent as death. She had panicked, started walking with her hands out in front of her, taking baby steps so she wouldn't run into anything. Then, all of a sudden, she found herself engulfed in the scent of fall.

It was the only way to describe the smell she'd been dreaming about her entire life. It smelled like fireplace smoke, cold air, leaves…and peppermint.

It was the oddest thing, but almost every nightmare she'd had in her twenty-four years had abruptly ended with a fog rolling in and that smell. It was as if, instead of a guardian angel, she had this guardian…mist. She didn't know how else to describe it. But whenever that scent came to her, whatever was worrying, frightening, or freaking her out just stopped, and she felt safe once more.

Rin had no idea what the dreams meant, but she didn't have time to figure it out at the moment. She had way too much to do, including emailing her half-sister back to reassure her she wasn't going to lose the ring. She also had to decide what she was going to wear for her birthday party…and think about when she could fit in a trip to England to meet her long-lost sister.

Weirdness, family curses, a lying mother, and the chance that she might die an old maid notwithstanding, today was a good day. She had found her sister. That meant the world to Rin.

# Chapter Two

"GIVE ME THE ring," Cassia demanded, holding out her hand impatiently.

Rin shook her head and put her hand in her pocket, protecting the amazing piece of jewelry. "No. I told you that as part of the agreement—that I signed and had to get *notarized*—I'm the only one who can wear it and I agreed that it would be sent back to England by next week."

"That's utterly ridiculous! It's *my* ring, I gave it to her in the first place, and that woman has no right to dictate who will wear it and where it will be stored," her mom said petulantly.

Rin gazed at her sadly. She'd held a glimmer of hope that when her mom realized she'd found MacKenzie, she'd be overjoyed that her child was alive and well. Rin had prayed that her half-sister might have been some-how…misinformed about what happened to her when she'd been an infant. But when Cassia had told Rin some convoluted story about how her first baby had ended up in a box outside of a fire station, which was obviously a ridiculous attempt at a lie, the fantasy died fairly quickly.

Her mom really *had* thrown away her daughter as if she were trash and had tried to get rid of the ring as well. Now it was back and Tina had to find her true love in less than a month.

"No, Mother. The ring is safe on my finger. Nothing is going to happen to it. When Tina finds her true love, it'll change colors no matter whose finger it's on. Now, talk to me about this party. What still needs to be done?"

Cassia huffed and Rin knew her mom was still pissed, but, thankfully, she let it go for now.

The ring was warm against Rin's finger, but even though it had a slight red glow when it had arrived (a residual glow from MacKenzie's love?), it was now back to the gray color Cassia said it had been when she'd seen it last.

"Fine. I don't understand why you're being difficult about it, but if Tina doesn't find her true love tomorrow night, I'm holding you responsible. And don't think you'll be able to avoid suffering right along with all of us. You're a part of this family. If the curse isn't broken, you'll be affected just as much as we are."

Rin ignored the threat, having heard it before and

honestly not caring anymore. It usually seemed to be her fault Tina couldn't find the man meant to be hers, for one reason or another. "The party, Mom?"

"Nothing. I don't need you to do anything. I've taken care of it all. Invitations went out on social media, I've personally talked to every influential man I can think of in the city with a son. Hell, I even went to the community college and put fliers up. Tomorrow night should be hopping with single, eligible men. Tina will find the man meant to be hers. I just know it."

Rin stopped the eye roll that threatened to escape just in time. How in the world her mom could even know Tina's true love would be living in Columbus, let alone show up at the party, was beyond her, but she knew better than to ask. Cassia had always been like this. Hard and tough, but ultimately still holding out hope that somehow Tina's one true love would materialize out of thin air.

"What time do you want me there?"

"You?"

"Yeah, Mom, *me*. For my birthday party?"

"Hmmm, yeah, well, it's mostly for Tina. You know, all the single guys and all. You can come and say hello, but since it's her party, you should probably just plan on being there for a short time. It wouldn't be good if you managed to catch the attention of a man who should be with Tina. I'll take some pictures of the two of you so people don't talk, but then you make yourself scarce."

"Mom," Rin complained in exasperation. "We're twins. I know Tina's your favorite, but it's ridiculous to not expect me to attend the entire night. You know people will be suspicious if I don't." Her mother's barbs didn't hurt anymore; she was too used to them.

"*Fine*. We'll mingle and chat at six then sit down to dinner at seven. Lights go down and the music starts at eight-thirty."

"Do you need anything beforehand? Help setting up?'

"No."

It was always like this. Rin was a part of the family, but only peripherally. "I'll be there around five, just in case."

"Varinia?"

"Yeah, Mom?"

"Thank you for finding the ring. I just want you to be happy, you know that, right? Tina is the key to making us *all* happy. That's all I'm trying to do here. That's all I've wanted for you both."

It was these small glimpses of love that her mom let slip through that made Rin not give up on the woman once and for all. "I know, Mom. I know." And Rin *did* know. She'd heard it enough over the years to understand that *everything* Cassia had done her entire life had been done to chase the elusive fairytale that was finding one's true love. Even favoring one twin over the other.

"See you tomorrow, Mom."

Cassia nodded absently, already back to thinking about the party the next day, and Rin headed out the door of her mom's house and to her car. She hadn't seen Tina; she was most likely at the spa being pampered before her big night.

Rin had worked eight hours that day and had another full day tomorrow. She was going in early to make sure she could finish the project she was working on before her party. Typically, Friday's were slow, so that would make getting the work done easier.

She was proud of how far she'd come since graduating high school. She'd earned her undergraduate degree in computer science and had lucked into a job at the same firm she'd interned with. She now worked in the IT department, improving the company's software and trying to come up with new and better reports for the employees. It wasn't glamorous, but Rin herself was anything but glamorous. The job fit her perfectly.

Whatever the outcome of the ring, whether by some miracle Tina met her true love tomorrow, or in the next couple of weeks before the actual date of their twenty-fifth birthday, Rin would soon be taking the first step toward the rest of her life...and she couldn't wait.

# Chapter Three

RIN SAT AT the back of the room and watched as Tina and her mom made the rounds to the different tables during dinner. Tina looked beautiful. Her auburn hair had been styled professionally and hung around her face in fat auburn curls that looked perfect. Her makeup was elegant and the dress she was wearing would put the famous Hollywood actresses on Oscar night to shame. It was an emerald green that complemented her hair perfectly and hugged her slender curves, somehow leaving nothing and everything to the imagination at the same time.

Of course, Rin had the same color hair, but it was cut short and, as usual, wouldn't behave, no matter what Rin did to it. When she wanted it to lie flat, it bounced up in curls; when she wanted it to be curly, it refused to cooperate. But she preferred her short hair. It stayed out of her face and eyes when she worked, and it was super easy to deal with when she worked out.

Rin could've borrowed something to wear from her sister, they were exactly the same size after all, but she wasn't sure Tina would loan her anything. Secondly, Rin was happy in her dress slacks and cashmere sweater. She'd gotten the latter for a steal last year and it was one of her favorite things to wear. It was a light yellow color and was as soft against her skin as it looked. She might not be as classically beautiful as her sister, but Rin was pleased with how she looked. And besides that, she was herself. A cocktail dress just wasn't something she was comfortable in.

The ballroom was beautiful; Cassia had outdone herself for the party. The woman might not win Mother of the Year, but she had an eye for decorating. There were small twinkling lights hanging from the ceiling and the green and gray color scheme really worked well in the large room. The tablecloths were gray, and the flowers on each table were white, gray and liberally stuffed with green. All-in-all, it was a lovely party, and Tina was in her element.

Rin truly was happy for her sister. She looked like she was enjoying herself, even with the curse hanging over her head, and that was the most important thing. She'd never wish Tina ill. Ever.

Cassia gestured to Rin, and she stood and headed over to her mother.

"Varinia, can you please go to the lobby and see if

you can't find the night manager? I'd like the wait staff to clear the tables a bit faster. Oh, and maybe see if they can get another bartender? The line is a tad bit too long."

Rin sighed and nodded. She'd been doing odd jobs for her mom all night. She assumed it was a ploy to get her out of the room, but in the end, she didn't really mind. Standing around watching Tina flirt wasn't exactly her idea of a good time.

She went through the maze of hallways to get back to the lobby and stood in line behind a man who was obviously checking in at the front counter.

Not paying much attention at first, thinking about something she needed to do at work the next week, Rin was startled when she realized the scent in the air was very familiar.

She tilted her head and breathed in again, deeper this time.

The man in front of her finished checking in and moved slightly to the side, throwing a leather bag over his shoulder. "Evening," he said in a polite tone, nodding and smiling at her as he turned in profile.

His movements wafted his delicious scent toward Rin once more, engulfing her senses, and shockingly, all she could think about was burying her face in the stranger's neck and breathing him in.

Smoke.

Cold air.

Leaves.

And when he'd said hello, she'd gotten a whiff of peppermint.

Freaking *peppermint.*

Rin's mind whirled. What in the world was going on? Who was this man and how could he smell *exactly* like the calming scent she'd dreamed about her entire life? She had the firm thought that if he put his arms around her, she could burrow in and he'd keep her safe from anything that might want to hurt her. It was insane, but she suddenly longed to feel that safety, just once before she died.

He was taller than her five-six by at least a couple of inches. He had dark, curly hair, a five-o'clock shadow on his square jaw, and beautiful hazel eyes. He was wearing a pair of jeans that had seen better days. Somehow Rin knew he hadn't bought the jeans with the holes strategically placed on his thigh and knee, as many people did these days. He looked too…masculine to care much about fashion. His shirt was a long-sleeve plaid Henley, which strained over the muscles in his arms.

She continued to openly study the man and tried to place him. He seemed familiar to her, but she couldn't remember Tina or her mom ever talking about a man who looked like him, so he probably wasn't there for the party. He looked as though he was in his mid-thirties, definitely too old to have gone to school with Tina. Paired with his relaxed clothes was a set of work boots, probably steel-toed. His fingers were long and one hand was still clutching the leather bag over his shoulder. The other was resting at his hip, his fingers tucked into the front pocket of his jeans…

And he was grinning at her, obviously amused rather than offended by her long stare.

"Hello?"

His single word made her snap back to herself. Jesus, he must think she was an idiot, standing there drinking him in as if she'd been stranded on a desert island. "Oh, sorry. I didn't mean to stare at you."

He kept smiling, but moved all the way aside so she could step up to the front desk. Aware that he wasn't walking away and was, in fact, standing close enough for Rin to get the occasional whiff of his delicious scent, but not close enough for him to be blatantly eavesdropping, she forced herself to meet the eyes of the bored-looking receptionist.

Focusing back on the task at hand, she relayed her mom's wishes regarding the party. The woman nodded and said she'd contact the night manager, who would get with the catering manager and take care of it.

Rin nodded and thanked the woman and turned— to see the man still standing nearby.

"Do we know each other?" the man asked when she faced him again.

"I don't think so. Do you know Tina Velt? Are you here for her party? We're twins, so maybe that's how you recognize me. Although we're pretty different."

"A party?" he asked.

"Yeah. It's a birthday thing."

"So, it's Tina's and *your* birthday party then," he said with a grin. The man held out his hand. "Neat. I'm Roman."

She looked at his hand for a long moment, somehow knowing without a doubt that her life would change if she took it. Finally, she stretched out her own, and as he took hold, said, "Varinia."

"Varinia? That's unusual."

Rin took a deep breath as Roman shook her hand. Goosebumps raced up her arm and down her spine at his touch. She could smell him even better now that they were standing so close and she *did* feel safe in his presence. A little flustered by how strongly she was attracted to the stranger, she told him, "Yeah, it's Latin. Means 'versatile.' My sister's name is actually Augustina, which means 'great.' She goes by Tina for short.

"Interesting names."

Rin nodded and reluctantly dropped the man's hand. But it did nothing to break her from the oh-my-God-is-this-man-beautiful-and-I-just-want-to-bury-my-nose-in-his-neck-and-never-leave haze she was in. "My mom's name is Cassia, Grandma's name was Juno, Great-Grandma was Maxima and Great-Great-Grandma's name was Marcellina."

She closed her eyes for a moment in embarrassment, realizing she'd just given him a mini Velt genealogy lesson that he in no way asked for.

"They're great names. And interestingly enough, my mom also had a thing for ancient-sounding names."

"Yeah?"

"Yup. You know I'm Roman. My brothers are Augustus and Maximus."

"Wow. That's so weird. Not your names, but the coincidence."

"We've got something in common, that's for sure. How long is your party going on tonight?" Roman asked.

Rin shrugged. "Until it's over. Knowing my sister and mom, probably late."

"Any chance, if I find presents for you and your sister, that I can be invited?"

"Are you single?"

"Uh, yeah…?" he said, as if wondering what that had to do with anything.

Rin's tummy did a summersault at the confirmation of his bachelorhood. "You're more than welcome to attend," she told him immediately, but quickly held up her hand to forestall him, and continued when it looked like he was going to say something. "Here's the thing: It's a really long story, one that you probably don't want to know, but my sister is looking for a husband. So you being single is present enough. The party's in the ballroom. No need to buy anything."

Roman opened his mouth to respond—or maybe it just dropped open in shock—but Rin continued on quickly again. "I know, it's ridiculous and crazy, but there it is. Most of the people at the party are men, that's why I thought you might have known Tina in the first place and you were here for the party. My dear twin is checking them all out in the hopes that she'll have an immediate connection with one and they'll live happily ever after, forever and ever. I'm kinda scared to sic her on you. You seem like a decent guy." She smiled to let him know she was teasing. "I'd hate for you to get sucked into her web. I love her, she's my sister, but she's…" Rin trailed off, searching for the right word.

"Not you," Roman finished for her with a straight face.

A full-blown shiver from her head down to her toes washed over Rin as she looked into Roman's eyes and saw his sincerity.

"You haven't seen Tina."

"But I've seen you…and I like what I see."

"Yeah, well, even though we're twins, she's much

prettier than I am. She has long hair and always wears clothes that make her look fabulous," Rin explained, figuring she might as well be honest.

She remained still, hypnotized, as Roman's hand came up to her face and tucked an errant curl behind her right ear. "There's no way she's prettier than you." His gaze traveled down her body then came back up to hers. "And what you're wearing is perfect. You look comfortable in your own skin. Classy. I like it."

"Oh." Rin wasn't sure what to say.

Roman dropped his hand but didn't move out of her space. "I've worked a long day. I walked into this hotel wanting nothing more than to get a room, take a shower, and relax on the bed while watching a football game and ordering room service. But suddenly, after meeting a wonderful woman who just happens to be in the middle of her own birthday party, I don't care about any of that. I'd like to spend some time with you, Varinia."

"You can call me Rin. Everyone does."

"I like Varinia. And I'm not everyone."

Wow.

The way he'd looked her in the eye when he said that made goosebumps crawl down her arms. She'd never reacted to anyone in her entire life the way she reacted to this man.

"Okay. But don't blame *me* when my mom makes

her move and decides you're Tina's fate."

"You'll be there to rescue me."

"I will?" Rin smiled at him. Roman was actually pretty funny. And he smelled so good. So comforting. So familiar.

"Yup."

"What is it that you do?"

"For a living?" Roman asked, tilting his head.

"Yeah."

"I'll tell you later. Over a piece of birthday cake," he said coyly.

Rin chuckled. "Fine."

"And you can tell me the really long story about why you think your twin sister is prettier than you."

Rin wrinkled her nose at that. "Uh, I'm not sure—"

"I'm still gonna go up to my room and clean the day off, but I'll be down in about twenty minutes. You'll wait for me?"

"Here?"

"No, not here," Roman chuckled and Rin blushed.

Duh. Of course not here. Jeez, she was a dork.

"I'll meet you in the ballroom," Roman told her.

"It's kinda hard to find, so I'll leave breadcrumbs," Rin told him with a straight face.

"I'd appreciate it," he responded immediately.

A man who seemed to get her weird sense of humor. Rin liked that. She began backing away from him and didn't see an ornate chair—and backed right into it, stumbling as she righted herself. She waved off the hand he held out, as if he was going to haul her against him to keep her upright.

She blushed. "Ha, sorry. I'm good. I'm just clumsy. I'll see you later, Roman."

"Later, Varinia."

She smiled at him and turned to head through the lobby. She looked back at the end of the large room and saw he was standing by a bank of elevators, still watching her. She waved awkwardly and disappeared around the corner.

Wow. The party might be for her sister, but Rin knew, without a doubt, that she liked Roman. He might be older than her. He might not be her true love—heck, she was probably never going to get that, according to the curse—but she could sure enjoy spending the evening with him at her party.

Rin hugged herself. She couldn't wait to see him again.

# Chapter Four

RIN GOT BACK to the ballroom to see that Tina and their mom were still making the rounds. Her sister was smiling and laughing and generally being her usual over-the-top happy self.

Rin fielded a few "happy birthdays" from some of the guests and found another table in a back corner and settled contentedly into a chair. There were two people sitting on the other side of the large circular table, but they were engrossed in a conversation and didn't try to include her. Rin got out her phone and pretended to be busy as she thought about Roman.

Now that she had a moment, she contemplated the amazing coincidence that she'd somehow dreamed about a smell her entire life—and it was the same scent that clung to Roman like a second skin. It was impossible, but somehow she knew it was true.

Then Rin remembered the ring for the first time that evening and lifted her right hand to look at it.

She gasped in surprise and blinked, trying to clear her eyes.

It was no longer the dark gray color it'd been since she'd put it on—it was now a deep crimson. Still almost black, but not quite.

She looked up suddenly, looking for Tina. Had her sister found her true love? Was that why it'd lightened? Good Lord, might the curse actually be lifting?

Tina was now sitting at a table with four men. They all seemed to be laughing and having a wonderful time. Her sister put her hand on the knee of the guy next to her and leaned into him. Rin tried to memorize what the four men looked like, so she could keep her eye on them. One of them *had* to be Tina's true love for the ring to react the way it had.

Cassia had sat Rin and Tina down when they'd started high school and she'd given them a history lesson about their ancestors. The legend of the ring had started with Theodosia and Lucius, back in the days when people wore togas. The names of others in her family swam in her brain as if she was sitting in front of her mom again, hearing them for the first time. Valeria and Tyren, Antonia and Titus, Valeriana and Aiden, Annie and Alex, and the most recent couple, Britannia and Charles.

Rin took a deep breath and closed her eyes, praying with all her heart that Tina would join her ancestors as the next woman who found true love before her twenty-fifth birthday. It would make a great story, one Tina could lovingly tell her own daughter when she was old enough to understand and appreciate it.

Even though they weren't close, Rin wanted that for her sister. She wanted her to follow in the footsteps of their long-deceased kin. She watched Tina flirt with and smile at the men at her table for a while, wondering which one might end up being her brother-in-law.

Just when Rin didn't think Roman was going to return, she somehow sensed him enter the large room.

She looked away from her sister's table and saw him standing in the doorway. Seeing him there made everything else in her mind disappear. Her only thought was to get to his side.

Rin stood up and headed in his direction, but wasn't paying attention to where she was going and completely missed a woman who was pushing away from a table. The chair suddenly appeared in her path and Rin swore under her breath as she tried to stop herself from falling over it—and failed.

It was a comedy of errors. The lady shrieked at finding Rin practically on top of her as she tried to stand, a man old enough to be her grandfather tried to grab Rin's arm to keep her from falling, and Rin herself jerked to the side to try to avoid the collision.

Her movements were enough to pull the older man

off his feet at the same time she pitched to the side. She fell against a nearby table, hitting her hip bone, and when the older man fell against her, got pushed to the ground by his weight.

They both lay sprawled on the floor of the ballroom, trying to catch their breaths.

"Jesus, Varinia, are you all right?" Roman asked. He'd rushed over, his brows drawn down in concern.

Rin closed her eyes in mortal humiliation.

She was clumsy. She'd been that way her entire life. Usually it wasn't that big of a deal, but going ass-over-feet in the presence of the first interesting man she'd met in ages wasn't big on her to-do list for the evening. It was inevitable that she'd trip, fall, bruise or otherwise make an ass of herself at some point, but doing it in front of the wonderful-smelling man sucked. The only good thing about the entire incident was that she wasn't wearing a skirt or dress. If she had been, she would've flashed everyone around them and they'd have gotten a way-too-personal glimpse of the red satin undies she'd worn for the special occasion.

Rin looked up and saw Roman helping the elderly gentleman off the floor as if he weighed less than a child. He was put on his feet, and Roman steadied him, keeping his hand on his elbow until he was stable again.

Rin slowly got to her feet, wincing at the ache in her hip but ignoring it. She'd had worse. "I'm good, thanks,

Roman. Told you I was clumsy." She turned to the stereotypical-looking grandpa she'd taken to the ground as if they were reenacting a WWE scene. "Are you okay? I'm so sorry, I didn't mean to take you to the ground with me."

"Heh. I think I'm the one who should be apologizing to you, young lady," he told her with a twinkle in his eye. "You probably could've righted yourself if I hadn't interfered and tried to help. I keep forgetting my strength isn't what it used to be."

An older woman snuggled up to the man, putting her arm around his waist in support. "Come on, Superman, how about we go and get a piece of that delicious-looking cake?" She winked at Rin. It was obvious the woman was trying to take the sting out of the fact that her man wasn't as strong as he used to be.

At that moment, Rin almost felt sad about her family curse. She'd never thought she needed a man to make her life complete or meaningful, and still didn't, but seeing how sweet the man and woman were to each other, and how protective, made a pang of jealousy streak through her.

"Varinia, are you sure you're all right?" Roman repeated, after the older couple and the woman who'd backed into her had left.

"I'm fine." Rin waved off his concern. At his look of disbelief, she insisted, "Happens all the time. I'll probably trip over my own feet at some point tonight."

When he still looked concerned, she conceded in a lower, more serious voice, "I'll most likely have a bruise. But I always have bruises. Nothing's broken, promise, it's all good."

She smiled to try to reassure him and was about to suggest they go and sit down to chat—until she saw her mom heading their way.

Her mom's man-dar was working overtime tonight and Roman was a fine specimen.

Rin looked over at him. He'd changed out of the torn jeans and long-sleeved Henley, and was now wearing a maroon polo with a pair of dark blue jeans, so dark they could almost be black. He had the same boots on he'd been wearing earlier, but obviously wasn't carrying his leather bag anymore. He looked good. Really good.

"Damn," Rin muttered, seeing her mom checking Roman out as she approached. She felt extremely protective of the man and even a bit…territorial. She turned her back to her mother and looked up at Roman. "My mom's on her way over here. I was going to wait a bit before introducing you, but—"

"Well, well, well…who do we have here?" Cassia purred as she reached their side.

Rin sighed, but did what was expected of her and turned to face her mom. "This is Roman…uh…"

"Reese. It's good to meet you." Roman held out his hand, and didn't even flinch as Cassia took hold of it with both of hers and patted it with way too much gusto.

"The pleasure is all mine," she gushed.

Rin held back the eye roll that wanted to come out at the simpering tone in her mom's voice. She hadn't been around Roman all that long, but she really didn't like the way Cassia was eyeballing him...as if he was a meal and she hadn't eaten in days.

"I don't think I've seen you around before."

Roman smiled and answered Cassia's implied question. "I'm a friend of Varinia's. She invited me. It's good to meet you."

"Oh, so you know Rin already. Great. Come on, you have to meet Tina. I can't believe Rin kept you a secret." Her mom widened her eyes a margin at Rin before turning her hundred-watt smile back to Roman.

Roman looked amused at Cassia's response, but took it in stride. "I'd be happy to meet the other birthday girl."

Rin reluctantly followed along behind Roman and her mother as she towed the poor man across the room to where Tina was sitting. More than once in the past, a guy Rin had liked had totally forgotten about her once he'd met her sister. She really, *really* didn't want that to happen this time. She hadn't gotten to talk much to

Roman yet, but knew without a doubt that she'd find him even more fascinating than she did already...if he didn't get enamored with her sister before she had a chance.

The trio arrived at the table where Tina was holding court with the group of men. Cassia stood next to her firstborn and totally ignored Rin.

"Tina, I'd like you to meet Roman. Rin invited him and I knew he just had to meet *you* while he was here."

"Roman," Tina said and nodded her head in greeting, holding out her hand as if she were the Queen of England, the man she was being introduced to a mere peasant.

Roman's lips quirked up in a smile, as if he was amused at Tina's reaction, but politely took her hand in his and shook it. "It's nice to meet you. Happy birthday."

"Thanks. Are you from around here?"

"Unfortunately, no." Roman looked up and caught Rin's eyes before he continued. "I'm only a few hours away though...not too far."

"Did you get some cake, Roman?" Cassia asked in a sugary-sweet tone. "I can get some for you, so you can sit for a while and get to know Tina. Rin, can you please go and find one of the caterers? I have a question."

Rin could see right through her mom's request. She didn't need to speak to any of the wait staff; she simply wanted Rin out of the way.

She turned to leave, figuring it was easier than butting heads with her mom, but Roman grabbed her hand and held on tightly, preventing her from walking away.

"It was nice to meet you, Tina. I hope you have a great night." He then turned to Cassia and answered her question. "I'm sorry, ma'am, but I promised Varinia I'd have a piece of her birthday cake with *her*, so if you will excuse us…" His voice trailed off, waiting politely for her permission, which he didn't really need in the first place.

Both Tina and Cassia looked surprised at his obvious brush-off, but Tina's lifelong training on how to be polite in any situation kicked in, and she smiled sweetly. "It's okay, I know how much Rin likes her cake. She never could resist sweets. Take your time and I'll talk to you later, after my sister goes up to her room. She always goes to bed early. She's kind of a party pooper."

Roman smiled, although Rin could tell it was forced, and nodded at both Tina and their mom, then they headed off to the table with the cake.

"Sorry about that," Rin murmured when Roman didn't say anything.

He didn't respond verbally, merely hooked the hand he was still holding around his biceps. He leaned forward and grabbed two plates of cake, along with a pair of forks, then turned and headed for the corner of the room where Rin had originally been waiting for him.

Rin kept her mouth shut as they walked, not able to read his mood and not knowing exactly what to say. He'd draped her hand around his arm, so she was quite close to him as they maneuvered their way through the tables and chairs in the room. Once again, she could smell his unique scent as they walked. It was faint, but even after his shower, he still somehow smelled like fall.

Rin wanted nothing more than to put her head on his shoulder and snuggle into him, inhaling the comforting scent that had taken her out of her nightmares for years. But she really didn't want him running screaming from the room, freaked out when she started sniffing him.

Roman put the slices of cake on a table and held out a chair for her. Rin sat, then watched as he pulled out his own chair and settled into it. He put an elbow on the table and leaned close, facing her.

"Let me first say that I had no 'immediate connection' with your sister, as you put it, and I'd much rather be sitting here with you than her."

Rin simply nodded, fascinated at the look of irritation on his face at her family's attempt to hook him up with Tina.

"Second, if you didn't look exactly alike, I don't think I would've ever guessed you were related."

She ignored the looks comment. She knew she didn't hold a candle to her prettier sister. "I'm sorry about that. My mom is really a good person; she's just had a weird life and feels as if Tina is her, and our, last chance to be happy. She goes overboard."

Roman didn't look appeased. His "hmmm" was noncommittal, and Rin somehow knew he was being diplomatic and not wanting to say anything really harsh about her relatives. He went on. "And so you know, what you eat when and what time you like to go to bed has nothing to do with me liking you. Maybe your sister was telling the truth and trying to somehow turn my attention, or maybe she was lying for the same reason, but regardless, I feel comfortable with *you,* Rin. I've enjoyed talking with *you.* I'm attracted to *you.*"

"She wasn't lying," Rin told Roman honestly. "You don't have to try to make me feel better for being a fuddy-duddy. I'm okay with it, honestly."

He chuckled. "You have a hard time taking a compliment, don't you?"

"That wasn't a compliment."

"I meant it as one. But obviously I'm rusty," Roman admitted a bit self-deprecatingly.

"You said you've been working all day. What do you do?" Rin knew her question came out of left field, but she wanted to steer the conversation away from herself, and what time she may or may not go to bed, and the fact that it seemed Roman was trying to flirt with her.

"I'm a wilderness guide."

"A wilderness guide?" Rin repeated, having no idea what the heck that was. The look on her face must have been comical, because Roman burst out laughing, and held out a fork to her so she could eat the cake he'd picked up for them.

"Yeah. I get hired to take people out into the great outdoors and teach them how to survive. I also run tours along the Appalachian Trail in the summers."

"I don't get it."

"Don't get what?"

"You get *paid* for that?"

"Yeah, Varinia, I get paid for it. You've never taken a tour and had a guide with you? Whitewater rafting? Hiking? Horseback riding? Anything?"

Rin laughed and took a bite of the cake. It was delicious, of course. As if Cassia would have anything less than orgasmic cake at the last-chance party for her daughter to find a man. "No. I'm not exactly an outdoorsy girl."

"Now that's a shame," Roman said, clearly teasing her. "Nature is beautiful and there are so many wonderful things to do outside. You've seriously never been camping?"

"In a tent? No. I've spent the night in my car when I had to drive cross-country once, but I don't think that counts."

"No, that doesn't count, and it definitely wasn't safe." He mock glared at her. "I'd love to take you on one of my overnight hiking trips to show you what you've been missing."

"Really? Um, I don't do nature very well."

"Then you haven't done nature with the right person."

How he could say something so innocent, but still make it sound dirty, was beyond Rin. And he was so smooth she couldn't tell if he was doing it on purpose or not. Even though she'd never had the urge to sleep outside with the bugs and in the heat, somehow she knew Roman would make it a completely different, and exciting, experience.

Feeling flustered, and trying to keep herself from agreeing on the spot to go camping with him—and do anything else he might want to do with her—she blurted out, "Where do you live? You told my sister you aren't from around here, but that could mean you're from tons of places…"

As if he'd been around her forever rather than the thirty or so minutes they'd spent together, he followed her train of thought easily. "Not too far. I live over in western Pennsylvania. I could've driven home tonight, but it's been a long day and I'm tired. I'd planned on getting a good night's sleep and heading back in the morning."

Rin was curious now. It wasn't every day she met a wilderness guide. Heck, she'd *never* met one. "There's not much that's nature-y about Columbus, Ohio."

"You'd be surprised how many hidden trails there can be in a city, but yeah, I wasn't hiking or anything today. I spent the day with a group of Girl Scouts. The troop leader hired me to show them some of the things that the Boy Scouts are learning. Apparently, some of the members in the group found out what their brothers were getting to do with *their* troops, and demanded the same thing. I got to show them how to tie knots, pitch tents, and recognize things like poison ivy and oak in the woods. It was awesomely fun, but I'm beat. I had no idea ten little girls could ask so many questions. I swear if I hear the word 'why' one more time, I'll scream." Roman smiled as he said it, so Rin knew he was teasing.

Every word out of his mouth made Rin want to get to know him better. "So I take it you don't have kids?"

"Nope. Never been married either. You?"

"No. Not even close. How old are you?" As soon as the question came out of her mouth, Rin was embarrassed. "Oh God, I'm sorry. Don't answer that, it was extremely rude."

Roman chuckled. "It's okay. It's only fair, since I know that you're twenty-five today. I'm thirty-four."

Rin grinned at him, happy she'd guessed his age

right earlier. Thirty-four was older than she thought she'd ever be attracted to, but it wasn't as if she wanted to jump a grandpa's bones, so she'd take it. "Actually, our birthday isn't for another couple weeks but Mom didn't want to chance it."

"Chance what?"

Lord. She hadn't meant to say that. "That long story I mentioned earlier, involving soul mates."

Roman relaxed against his chair. "It's not like I have anywhere else to be. Hit me."

"I don't want to. I'm liking this."

"This?"

"Us, talking normally, without you looking at me like I'm an escapee from the looney bin."

"Come on, Varinia, it can't be that bad. I'm sure I could tell you some things about me that would freak you out just as much."

"Like what?"

He considered her for a moment before confessing in a low voice, as if there were other people around who would love to hear what he was about to tell her, "I used to sneak out of bed at night when I was little to watch princess movies. I don't know why we had them, since I don't have any sisters, but I loved them."

Rin gawked at Roman for a moment. He looked so sheepish that she couldn't help the guffaws of laughter that escaped her. She laughed so hard she actually snorted, then covered her face in embarrassment. Could she be any more of a dork?

At his chuckle, she looked up and sighed, still smiling. "Okay, okay. I think that's more sweet than embarrassing though. But you fessed up, so I will too. But I'm only doing it because in another few weeks, it won't matter anyway."

Roman put his hand on her forearm and said seriously, "If you really don't want to tell me, don't. It's fine. I don't think anything you could say right now would make me think less of you. In case you haven't realized it, I like you. It probably sounds creepy, but from the second I saw you standing behind me in the lobby, I've been drawn to you. And I don't know what happens in a few weeks, but I really hope that whatever it is *we* have lasts longer than that. Talk to me."

"Uh, well, okay." Rin took a deep breath and asked what she'd been thinking since she'd first gotten close enough to Roman to smell him; again, the question seemingly coming out of the blue. "You asked me in the lobby if we'd met before."

Roman nodded but didn't speak, letting her get whatever it was she wanted to say out at her own speed.

"I know we haven't, but the thing is, I feel like I know you from somewhere," Rin insisted, putting off telling the story of her family legend.

"Wanna hear something weird? I do too, it's why I

asked earlier. But I swear I've never laid eyes on you before in my life. There's no way I would've forgotten you."

Ignoring the warm and gushy feeling she got from his words, Rin asked, "Maybe you met Tina and just forgot? We *are* twins, so even though she looks different from me, you know, with her hair and her clothes and stuff, we're still identical."

"No, I haven't met her either," Roman denied. "And while she might look different, I'd be able to tell you apart even if you had the same haircut and were wearing the same clothes. You look pretty much exactly alike, from your beautiful green eyes to your cute nose and full lips, but there's just something about you that makes you very different from Tina."

"Oh. Um. Thanks."

"There goes that not-accepting-a-compliment-very-well again." Roman reached out a hand and ran a finger over her cheek briefly before pulling back. "I'm drawn to you and it's not about anything that Tina also has. This is gonna sound corny but...it's as if my soul recognized yours."

Rin could only stare at him. She felt her heart speed up.

That was it exactly.

Before she could respond, he asked the question that wasn't all that much of a subject change since they'd been talking about souls. "Now…long story about Tina trying to find her true love?"

"Okay, um, yeah. But you can't tell anyone here. It would embarrass both Tina and my mom."

"Of course. I know we just met and you don't know me at all, but I wouldn't break your confidence."

Rin took a deep breath and began the crazy story. "It all started thousands of years ago with a woman named Theodosia and her husband, Lucius…"

# Chapter Five

"IT'S AMAZING THAT the ring has been passed down for hundreds of years from mother to daughter," Roman said in awe, as if trying to wrap his mind around the possibility.

"I know. Some of the stories about my ancestors I remember, but I know lots of others are lost, which makes me sad. The thing is, though, for some reason, it's been…broken, for lack of a better word, for the last few generations, and why my mom calls it a curse now instead of a legend. My great-grandmother, grandmother, and mother weren't lucky enough to find their true loves by the time they were twenty-five."

"But they still had daughters," Roman remarked.

Rin looked at him with a raised eyebrow. "You don't exactly have to be in love to have kids you know."

Roman nodded his head in sheepish agreement. "Good point. So Tina has only a few more weeks to find the love of her life, otherwise she, and you, will be single for the rest of your lives?"

Rin read the disbelief in his tone and blushed. It sounded so silly when he said it out loud. This was the reason she hadn't bothered to try to explain it before. But something about Roman had made her think he'd understand. "Basically, yes." There was no use in expanding her answer if he was going to think she was crazy.

"That is utterly fascinating," Roman said enthusiastically, resting both elbows on the table in front of him and keeping his eyes on hers.

Rin watched as his biceps flexed under the short-sleeve polo shirt he was wearing. She took a deep breath, inhaling his unique scent as he shifted next to her.

"And you said that you have an older half-sister who lives in England who sent the ring? Is Tina wearing it now? I'd love to get a look at it…that is, if we can figure out a way to do that without making your sister think I'm her true love."

Roman seemed genuinely interested and Rin made a split-second decision. She brought her right hand up from where she'd stuffed it under her thigh and rested it on the table between them. "I've got it. I didn't trust my mom not to do something weird with it. She already tried to get rid of it once, and I promised MacKenzie, my half-sister, that I'd keep it with me at all times."

Roman reached out to lift her hand, but stopped, his

fingers hovering over hers, and asked permission before touching her, and thus the ring. "May I?"

Rin swallowed hard and nodded. "Legend says that when the eldest daughter finds her true love, it turns crimson, but my mom says it's been gray for as long as she's had it."

Rin held her breath and Roman picked up her hand. She shivered as his thumb brushed over the back of her hand as he pulled it closer to examine the ring. He turned her hand one way, then the other. Rin felt his warm, calloused fingers over hers, but couldn't take her eyes off his face. It was extremely expressive. She could see curiosity, interest, and...confusion?

"What's wrong?" she asked.

"It's probably a coincidence, but I swear I've seen this ring before. You wouldn't believe me if I told you."

"Try me," Rin breathed.

"Later. You said the ring is supposed to be black. But it's not. It's a dark red right now."

"What?" Rin looked down at the antique for the first time since she'd sat down with Roman. She gasped in surprise. She'd thought it was more red than black earlier, but now she couldn't deny it. The ring was definitely crimson and seemed to glow from within. It was the most beautiful stone she'd ever seen in her life.

"I-I don't understand," Rin stammered, looking away from her finger to search the room for Tina. She saw her sitting with two of the men she'd been chatting with earlier. She was laughing and smiling at them both.

She turned back to Roman. "I think it might actually be working."

He smiled at her with a gleam in his eye. "Oh, it's working all right."

Rin was too excited and flabbergasted to catch the odd tone in his voice. "I'm afraid to believe. I'm so happy for her. She's been wanting this her entire life. I should go tell my mom—no, I should wait. I wouldn't want to get her hopes up in case something goes wrong. Mom would love to see the ring this color though. Oh, Roman, this is amazing!"

He squeezed her hand and brought it up to his lips, kissing the ring on her finger. She could feel the heat from his lips against her skin, and shivered as a burst of energy seemed to flow from her fingers, up her arm, and settle in her chest. She felt jittery, as if she'd just downed an energy drink, and warmth spread out from her heart to all four of her limbs.

Roman didn't say a word, but if the look in his eyes was any indication, he'd somehow felt the same thing.

"Think you could get out of here for a bit? Take a walk with me?"

He hadn't let go of her hand and Rin couldn't take her eyes off his lips. "I shouldn't. This is an important—no, *momentous* thing for our family. But…" Rin looked longingly at the door to the ballroom. She wanted to be alone with Roman. She needed it, as if she needed to breathe. She didn't understand it, but she wanted to say yes more than anything. However, she was also cautious. She'd just met the man tonight, after all. "A walk? Is that code for something else?"

He chuckled and put her hand back on the table, covering it, and the ring, with his own. "No. I'd just like to spend some time with you, get to know you better, have you get to know *me* better. It's loud in here and I'd love to talk to you without distractions…if you think you can leave your own birthday party."

"I was going to cut out soon anyway. So yes, I'd like that."

Roman smiled at her, obviously pleased she'd said yes. "I'll make sure to keep you safe. Thank you for trusting me." Roman stood up and kept hold of her hand, forcing her to stand as well. He dropped it, only to rest his warm palm on the small of her back as they walked toward the ballroom door.

Rin's head spun. Roman's scent, his seeming interest in her, the ring being crimson for the first time ever…it was all almost too much. But walking next to Roman, being by his side, felt right. She'd follow him to the ends of the earth if he asked.

# Chapter Six

THEY MADE THEIR way out of the hotel and headed for the downtown area. The neighborhood was well lit and the fountains around the courthouse gave their surroundings a romantic feel. Roman had taken hold of her right hand, interlocking their fingers. Rin looked down and saw the poesy ring shining brightly in the streetlamps as they walked, flanked by his fingers.

They were quiet for a while, reveling in each other's company. Roman finally broke the comfortable silence. "Want a mint?" He'd reached into his pocket and was holding a tin of candy in his free hand, holding it out to her. "I'm totally addicted to them. My family makes fun of me, but I can't remember a time I wasn't."

"Are they peppermint?" Rin asked, even though she knew the answer already.

"Yeah. I've tried the wintergreen ones, and cinnamon, but I always come back to peppermint." He shrugged a little self-consciously. "It's a quirk."

She shook her head and let go of his hand so he could pop one of the small mints into his mouth. He immediately took hold of her hand again as soon as the tin was back in his pocket.

Rin inhaled deeply, smelling the familiar scents of smoke, cold air, and now peppermint. She felt like she was losing her mind. It couldn't be possible to have dreamt of Roman her entire life, but the proof was walking next to her and was holding her hand tightly. She decided to find out more about him, using his own words to further the conversation. "Will you tell me more about your family?"

"Sure. You know I have two brothers. We grew up outside Pittsburgh. My parents are still together, they're celebrating their thirty-fifth anniversary this year."

"Wow, that's a long time." Rin knew she sounded wistful, but couldn't help it. Roman squeezed her hand.

"They haven't all been happy, though. There was a time, when my youngest brother was in college, when Mom moved out. They had to work through some things. I think having three boys in the house kept them so busy that they didn't concentrate on their own relationship. So when all of us left and it was only the two of them, things got weird."

"But they worked it out?"

"Yeah." Roman nodded. "Thankfully. They love each other, but they had to learn how to be a couple

63

again rather than just a mom and a dad."

"You're lucky."

"I know," he agreed without hesitation. "But even if they would've gotten divorced, it wouldn't have changed the way they felt about us."

Rin nodded and said wistfully, "I never knew my dad. Mom said he was a one-night stand that resulted in us." She shrugged. "I don't know if he even knows he's got two daughters."

"I'm sorry, Varinia. He's missing out."

"Yeah, I know, but I think we missed out too. I love my mom, and I know, if asked, she'd admit to making a lot of huge mistakes in her life."

"But?"

"You could tell there was a but, huh?" Rin remarked dryly.

"Yeah, I could tell. I feel like I can read you pretty well. Sounds nuts, I know." Roman shrugged.

Rin squeezed his hand, letting him know she felt the same way, and went on. "My mom has always been obsessed with the legend of the ring. I told you about my half-sister. Mom literally dumped MacKenzie, and the ring, in the hopes that it would end the curse once and for all. But it didn't. So before me and Tina were born, she had a dream about the ring and the legend, and she's spent the last twenty-five years grooming Tina to find the love of her life."

"Can you groom someone for that?"

Rin shrugged immediately. "I have no idea. But if anyone could, it'd be my mom."

They walked on in silence for a moment, before Roman asked gently, "And you?"

"Me what?"

"What were you doing while Tina was being groomed?"

"Growing up," Rin told him honestly. "I was mostly left alone. I was allowed to read books as much as I wanted, I could play video games in front of the TV instead of going to ballet lessons. Mom gave me a little money to buy school clothes, although most of it I earned myself, and let me shop by myself instead of her picking out my clothes. I went to a great public high school, where I could blend into the woodwork and not have to worry about being a cheerleader or one of the cool kids."

Roman stopped and turned to Rin, not letting go of their intertwined hands. He put his free hand on her face. "So you were left to your own devices while Tina got all of your mom's attention."

"Yeah, I guess. But Roman, don't feel sorry for me. I had a safe childhood and I now do what I love—work with computers."

"Boyfriends?"

"What?"

"Boyfriends. Did you have them growing up?"

"Well, yeah, of course," Rin told him with a raised eyebrow. "I even dated this one guy for two years. He was the captain of the yearbook club and I thought I was in love with him."

They started walking again.

"What happened?"

"Nothing dramatic. He was a year older than me and he graduated and went on to college and hooked up with a swimmer. A junior."

"You don't sound heartbroken about it."

"Nope. It wasn't meant to be. What about you? I bet you had a ton of girlfriends in high school."

"Actually, I didn't. I thought girls were icky until I was around sixteen."

Rin laughed. "Icky?"

"Yup. I think I was traumatized by walking in on my father making out with my mom when I was ten."

"Yeah, that'd do it. But since then?"

"I've had my fair share. But I'll tell you something."

When he paused, Rin looked up. "What?"

"I've never felt about *any* of them the way I'm feeling right now. It's crazy, I know it is. We just met. But I feel comfortable with you. I already admitted that I used to watch girly princess movies and I have no problem telling you that I used to fantasize about being Prince Charming."

"From Cinderella?"

"Yup. It was my favorite."

Rin giggled, then sobered. She looked up at the stoplight instead of at him as they waited to cross a street. She still felt the jolts of electricity in her limbs and stomach. It was insane, but it also felt right. "So, you're the oldest?"

Roman allowed her to change the subject, as if he knew the topic was making her antsy. "Yeah, Augustus is the youngest and Maximus is the middle child."

Rin chuckled again at his brothers' names.

Roman smiled as he steered her around a group of people who'd just come out of a bar, preventing a collision. "Yup. My parents were a bit too into Roman history, kinda like you and your ancestors. They go by Gus and Max."

Rin shook her head in amusement. Weren't they a pair, with her own family's romanticized names. "Are they married?"

"Yes. Both to great women. They each have two kids."

"Please tell me they didn't name their kids Caesar or Julius."

Roman nudged her with his shoulder. "No. They have perfectly normal names. John, Lee, Timothy, and Stephanie."

"How old are they?"

"Gus' two are seven and five, and Max's are six and two."

"So…Uncle Roman?"

He chuckled. "Yup. I love those little stinkers. But I'm also really glad to get back to my empty house too. Kids are exhausting."

Rin smiled and teased, "Yeah, you said that already."

"Well, it's true. You have much experience with kids?"

Rin shook her head. "No, not really."

"So you work with computers. What exactly do you do for a living? Hack into top-secret databases?"

She snorted. "Nothing so exciting. I work in an IT department for a large company."

"I bet you're still a computer genius," Roman teased.

"No, not even close. But I do everything from removing viruses from computers to setting up new workstations."

"You really *aren't* an outdoors person, are you?" Roman asked seriously.

Rin shook her head a little sadly. "I'm not, but that doesn't mean that I don't *like* to be outside. I just haven't had the chance to do much. Growing up, my mom…well, you already know that she spent a lot of time with Tina, trying to make sure she was prepared to do whatever she could to find the man meant to be hers.

She didn't have a lot of time for 'boy things.'as she called them."

Roman was silent for a moment, as if he was trying to find the right way to say what he was thinking. Finally, he asked in a quiet voice, "What if the legend is wrong?"

Rin stopped walking and stared up at Roman in shock. They'd walked around the courthouse twice and were really just killing time. She was enjoying getting to know more about him and hearing about his family. But his words came out of left field. "What?"

"What if it's wrong?"

"It's not."

He didn't say anything, but continued to stare at her.

"Seriously, Roman. You've seen the ring. It's not wrong."

He pulled and encouraged her to start walking again. The night was cool, but not cold, and the darkness around them made it seem more intimate somehow.

"Here's the thing. You said it was the oldest daughter who got the ring, right?"

"Uh-huh. Tina pushed and shoved her way out of my mom first, so she got the short end of the stick, in my eyes." Rin wasn't sure where Roman was going with his questioning, but since he didn't immediately laugh or scoff at the story about the legend earlier, she was willing to hear him out.

"I'm still not clear on how the ring worked for your half-sister, who was *really* your mom's eldest daughter, but now it's supposed to work again for your twin, who isn't technically the oldest, but is the oldest with another man."

Rin sighed in relief. He wasn't mocking her, he was just confused. "Honestly? I'm not either, but MacKenzie trusted me enough to send it to me, and you've seen it for yourself. It's not gray anymore; it has to be true. One of those guys Tina was with tonight has to be her true love."

"So, your sister was born first."

"Yup."

"By how long?"

"How many minutes?"

When Roman nodded, Rin told him, "Not minutes. About thirty seconds."

"And you're *sure* she's the oldest?"

Rin stopped abruptly again, next to a bench this time. "Yeah, Roman. She's the oldest. The nurses marked her ID bracelet when she was still in the nursery so my mom would know who came out first. What are you getting at?"

"Can we sit?" Roman gestured at the wooden bench next to them.

Rin nodded and sat at the edge of the bench, suddenly uneasy at what Roman was implying. He turned toward her and took both of her hands in his and held them tightly.

"Here's the thing. I'm not a very spiritual man. And I've lived my life without much thought to the supernatural and legends and stuff. But the second I met you, I felt…different. As if I was just where I was supposed to be. Maybe I chose that hotel at random, or maybe I was guided to it for a reason. But the first time I touched you, I swear to God, my heart skipped a beat. I've never believed in love at first sight, but something happened between us.

"What if the legend applies to both of you? Or the nurses made a mistake and *you're* really the oldest? Or for this generation, it applies to all the daughters of your mom?"

Rin didn't know what to say, but it didn't matter as he continued on enthusiastically.

"You said it yourself, when you got the ring it was gray, but now it's not. It's bright red, beautiful. What if *we're* meant for each other and it changed colors because *you* met *me*?"

It was impossible.

But somehow, it wasn't.

"When I was little, I had nightmares," Rin told him. "Varinia—"

She held up a hand to forestall his comment. "It's related. Promise."

He nodded and gestured for her to continue.

"They were awful. My earliest memory is of waking up after a bad dream. I was probably three or so. I don't always remember what they're about, but all I know is that I'm lost, or surrounded, or trapped, or being chased, or somehow threatened. I'm scared out of my mind…but then a misty fog rolls in. It surrounds me, and should scare the crap out of me *more*, if that's possible. But it's as if it's putting itself between me and whatever it is that's frightening me in my dreams. It forms a barrier between me and the bad thing in my nightmare. It wraps itself around my legs, then my waist, then my chest…and instead of smothering me, it comforts me. It's like a warm blanket wrapped around me, keeping me safe."

"I think most children have those kinds of dreams. I know my niece and nephews have them."

"The fog that envelops me smells like smoke. Like a cold fall day. Like *peppermint*. It smells exactly like *you* do, Roman."

He didn't say anything to her absurd statement, just stared into her eyes before bringing his hand up and palming the side of her head. Rin closed her eyes and rested her head against his hand, letting him take her weight for a moment. She swallowed hard then looked up at him.

Roman was leaning forward, his face very close to her own. She bit her lip but didn't say a word. A million thoughts were running through her head. It *was* weird that the ring was now crimson, but her entire life she'd been told that Tina was the important daughter. Tina was the oldest. Tina was the key to breaking the curse.

But here, with Roman, she suddenly wasn't sure about anything anymore.

"I want to kiss you, Varinia." Roman's voice was low and rumbly.

Rin nodded her head infinitesimally, but knew he felt it because he licked his lips as if readying himself for her.

She copied his movements and waited.

He didn't leave her waiting long. Before she could take another breath, his lips were on hers. His hand curled around the back of her head, directing her to tilt it a bit more so the angle was better. Rin had half-expected him to give her a small peck, but was pleasantly surprised when he didn't bother with preliminaries. His tongue caressed her lips and when she opened for him, surged inside as if he'd done it a thousand times instead of just once.

His delicious scent seeped into her pores as he kissed her, a thousand times stronger than if she'd simply sniffed him. The mint he'd eaten earlier was still fresh on his breath and she could also somehow taste the wood smoke that permeated every fiber of her being. She inhaled as their tongues dueled, bringing his delicious scent into her lungs and shivering at the lust that coursed through her.

That was new.

In the past, in her dreams, his scent had always calmed her, but she felt anything but calm now. She could feel the arousal coursing through her veins. Her nipples tightened and she shifted in her seat, trying to douse the flames between her legs.

She wanted this man.

And if the way he shifted was any indication, so he was as close as could be as he kissed her, he felt the same way.

Rin's arms wrapped around his back and her fingers dug into his shirt. She moaned as he sucked on her tongue and again when he pulled back, letting them both catch their breaths as he nibbled on her bottom lip. Roman brought his hand up to the other side of her head and held her still in front of him.

"Remember when I said earlier that I thought I'd seen your ring before?" He waited until she nodded before continuing. "I've never dreamed, not like you," he said in a soft, reverent voice, "but the night before last, I woke up in the middle of the night after the most amazing, vivid dream I'd ever had. It was something about castles and swords, and I swear I'm not lying about this, but at the end, after I'd slayed the fire-breathing dragon, my reward was a princess. A red-haired princess with a pixie haircut and a smile that lit up the room. She held her hand out to me and as I reached for it, I realized I was holding something."

"What?" Rin whispered, almost scared to hear what he'd say.

"A ring. If I'm not mistaken—that exact ring you have on your finger. It was dull in my hand, but when I pushed it down her finger, it glowed the brightest red I've ever seen. The princess turned to me and said 'with dreams only of you,' and then she disappeared in a puff of smoke."

Rin felt the blood drain from her face and she pulled back from Roman. "That's not funny. Who have you been talking to? Did my mother put you up to this?"

Not understanding her tone and change in demeanor, Roman held his hands up in front of him in capitulation. "I swear on the lives of my niece and nephews, I'm not lying to you, and before tonight, I didn't know you or anyone in your family, Varinia."

"There's an inscription on the ring," Rin told him shakily. "It's in Latin, but MacKenzie told me what it meant."

"What's it say?" He asked the question, but it seemed he already knew the answer.

"You know."

"Tell me."

"*With dreams only of you.*"

Roman breathed out a minty breath and closed his eyes for a moment, as if he too was memorizing the moment. His eyes opened and Rin could see the honesty, the desire he had for her, the utter lack of guile in his gaze before he spoke. His hands gathered hers back into his grasp and he squeezed lightly.

"Varinia. I don't know how it happened, but I'm *him*. I'm the man who was made for you."

Rin shook her head in denial and confusion. What was happening here?

"You said it yourself; you've been dreaming about me your entire life. I don't know why or how. Maybe the legend is wrong; maybe, as I said before, you and your sister were somehow mixed up in the nursery after you were born. You *are* identical twins after all, but however it happened, you're mine. Mine to love. Mine to protect. I don't care about any legends. I'm not giving you up after your twenty-fifth birthday. Not even forty-eight hours ago, I dreamed of you. *You* are the princess I've been fantasizing about my entire life."

Rin felt like she was going to faint and Roman must've realized it. He reached for her and pulled her into his embrace, wrapping his arms around her and tucking her head into his shoulder. "Take slow breaths before you hyperventilate, Varinia."

She did as he suggested and immediately felt even more lightheaded at his delicious scent. She buried her nose further into his neck and inhaled, trying to bring it into her lungs. Then groaned. She felt her nipples harden once again and she shifted against him restlessly. A sense of safety and calmness came over her, on the heels of the lust. God, she felt more loved and safer than she'd ever felt, right here in Roman's arms. A man she'd met not even three hours ago.

It was insane, but Rin couldn't deny that it felt like she was home.

They stayed like that for a couple of minutes, not wanting to move. Finally, Rin pulled out of his grasp, just enough to look him in the eyes.

"I don't understand anything about this. All I know is that my dreams have been only of you for as long as I can remember. You've always been there for me. Always. I'm afraid this is all a mistake and in couple weeks, after I turn twenty-five, I'm going to lose you, as my mom has warned would happen if Tina didn't find her true love, no matter what you say tonight."

Roman opened his mouth to respond, but a voice behind them interrupted before he could get out whatever it was he'd wanted to say.

"Give me your wallets or I'll blow your goddamn heads off."

# *Chapter Seven*

R IN FROZE IN Roman's arms, eyes wide. They both turned their heads to see a man standing behind them. He was wearing jeans and a black hoodie that was pulled low over his forehead. He was wearing black gloves and had a gun pointed at them. When he bared his teeth, Rin could see they were crooked and stained. It was obvious, even to her, that he was a long-time drug user of some sort.

He was beyond scary looking and that was even before Rin looked down the barrel of the gun that was pointed at her face.

Rin's mind blanked. She had no idea what to do. Hell, she didn't even *have* her wallet on her. It was in her purse back in the ballroom. She hadn't even thought about bringing it with her when she'd left earlier with Roman.

Just as she began to panic, Roman spoke. "Easy, man. You can have it." He held up his hands to show he was unarmed and the loss of his arms around her made Rin shiver.

"No funny business or I'll blow a hole through your girlfriend," the thug warned.

Roman didn't so much as look at her, but kept eye contact with the man with the gun and slowly moved one hand to the back of his pants to grab his wallet. He slid it out of his pocket and instead of handing it over, opened it and pulled out the meager number of bills that were in there. He held them out to the man.

"Here. It's all the cash I've got on me."

The gun didn't waver as the guy snatched the money out of Roman's hand. "Credit cards too," he snarled.

Again, with no hesitation, Roman did as the man asked, pulling three credit cards out of their slots in his wallet and passing them over.

Thinking this was going to be over soon, the fastest robbery in history, Rin felt herself breathing deeply in slight relief.

Then the man with the gun turned to her. "Yours too, bitch."

"I don't have my purse with me. I'd give the whole thing to you if I had it. Swear." The response was immediate and genuine. The last thing she wanted to do was get in an argument with this guy. She would've had no problem handing it over if she had it. Life was too short and suddenly held too much promise to worry about trying to save a couple bucks.

"Don't fuck with me!"

"She's not," Roman tried to reassure the man quickly. "We left the hotel back there without it. We're just talking a walk."

The man's eyes narrowed on them. Rin had no idea what he was looking for. She was wearing black slacks and her yellow cashmere sweater that was way too dressy to be hanging out on this bench in the city, but was completely appropriate for the celebration going on a couple blocks away. Roman looked just as firmly middle-class. They weren't wearing expensive watches or jewelry.

As soon as the thought entered her mind, the man barked out, "Give me that ring then."

Rin couldn't help it. The thought of losing their family legacy, of letting MacKenzie down—who'd only loaned it to her, telling her a little of the story about how long it'd taken for the ring to be paired back up with some mysterious sword—made her put her other hand over her fingers, as if hiding the ring from the thief would do any good.

She shook her head in horror. "No, please. It's been in my family for thousands of years."

"All the more reason to hand it over, bitch." The scary man in the hoodie waved the gun at Roman. "Unless you want me to kill him."

Rin couldn't breathe. A minute ago she'd begun to think she'd found everything she'd ever wanted in her life. But now, she was afraid it was going to be taken from her before she'd even had it in the first place.

Roman's life was way more important than the poesy ring. She'd choose him over the jewelry every day and twice on Sunday. Every single time.

She started tugging at her finger, looking down at the ring, which was still glowing crimson. The tears in her eyes made everything blurry and she frantically tried to remove the ring. But of course, the damn thing seemed to be glued to her finger. She couldn't get it past her knuckle. Tears sprang to her eyes as she tried to force it off.

"Come on, you've got my money, take it and go," Roman tried to reason with the man.

"Give it, bitch!" the man snarled.

"I'm trying! It's stuck," Rin sobbed, tugging harder at the ring.

Rin looked up at the thief. His eyes held not one shred of humanity. They were cold, dark, and deadly.

She knew without a doubt that he was going to kill one or both of them. Even if she gave him the ring, she somehow sensed they were both going to die anyway.

Despite knowing that, she still tried to remove the poesy ring. She swung her gaze to Roman. He wasn't looking at her, as she'd hoped. She needed to see what she now knew was love in his eyes, once more before she died.

No, Roman's gaze was fixed on the gun.

Rin pulled hard at the ring, and as usual, her clumsiness got the best of her. She jerked to the side and hit her elbow on the back of the bench. Her movements were enough to startle the man with the gun and he took a small step backward.

It was as if time slowed down. Rin felt just like she was in one of her nightmares. She recognized the helpless feeling, the sense of doom. She opened her mouth to protest what she sensed Roman was about to do, but she was too late.

He launched himself over the back of the bench as if he'd done it every day of his life. Rin heard the pistol go off, then grunts as the men fell onto the concrete behind the bench. Roman was on top of the punk and they were both struggling for control over the gun.

A screech came out of her mouth and she looked around frantically for something to help Roman with. Seeing nothing, not even a piece of trash she could use to try to bash the bad guy's head with, she started screaming for help, hoping one of the few people they'd seen as they'd been walking would come and investigate or call for the police.

The fight continued in front of her, and Rin heard Roman telling her to run, but she couldn't. Her feet were glued to the ground. She didn't want to stay, but she couldn't leave.

For a moment, it looked like the thug was going to get the upper hand, but Roman was a big man, and strong. He punched him hard, twice.

After the third punch in the face, the man in the hoodie finally went limp under Roman.

It had all happened so fast, but Rin still felt as if everything was in slow motion. Roman eased himself off of the guy and whipped his head around at the same time, obviously trying to find her. When he saw her, his shoulders relaxed just a bit. "You okay?" His voice was low and gravelly. He had a trickle of blood coming out of the side of his mouth where the thug must've gotten in a lucky hit.

Rin nodded wordlessly, too shocked by the fog that seemed to be rolling in around her. The wispy smoke curled around her feet, but instead of crawling up her body, like it usually did in her dreams, it continued across the four or so feet separating her from Roman and started winding its way around *his* body.

He didn't seem to notice the weird smoke. He turned back to the bench, and Rin, and looked down at the ground, under where they'd been sitting together minutes earlier. Roman, still on his knees next to the man who'd tried to kill him, leaned over and picked something up off the ground.

Rin kept her eyes on his face and the smoke that had now risen to envelop his upper body. She jolted with his next words.

"My reward."

Rin looked down at the hand Roman was holding out to her. The poesy ring was resting in his palm, glowing bright crimson.

It must've finally popped off in her struggle to remove it when she'd fallen against the back of the bench and she hadn't noticed in the melee that had followed.

Rin remembered what she and Roman had been talking about before they'd been robbed. His dream. The princess. Slaying the dragon.

As he knelt on the ground in front of her, his arm outstretched, holding the ring, he looked exactly like the prince he'd aspired to be his entire life. *Her* prince. Her man.

Roman coughed and then Rin heard a gurgle. Her eyes flew up to his in alarm.

"Call the police, Varinia. If he comes to, I won't be able to do anything about it."

With those words, Roman tilted to the side, caught himself with his hand, then fell the rest of the way to the pavement and rolled over to his back, still coughing weakly.

The weird smoke stayed with him as he fell and formed a sort of see-through blanket over his torso.

"Roman!" The word was merely a breath of air out of Rin's lungs, but he heard her. His head turned to her as she scrambled to his side. A small dark stain was spreading on the right side of his chest. Not knowing what else to do, Rin put both hands over it and pressed down, hard. "Don't die, Roman! Oh my God, please. Don't leave me alone. I just found you. You *are* him. I don't know how it happened but somehow it did. Please…"

Roman groaned as her hands pressed into the gunshot wound and he grimaced. But his eyes stayed on hers as he spoke, his voice tortured and pained. "When I was sixteen, I wrote a poem. It's awful, but I was compelled to write it. Now I know why."

The tears fell unchecked down Rin's cheeks as she listened to the only man she'd ever love whisper the most amazing words she'd ever hear. She didn't pay attention to the sirens in the background, nor the people who were coming out of the shadows of the night to help deal with the thug on the ground next to them. She only saw Roman. Only heard his words.

He coughed once, more blood coming up from his lungs, then reached up and grabbed hold of one of her hands. He tugged at it, and Rin, not wanting to hurt him further, allowed him to remove it from his chest. She kept the other hand where it was, trying to keep any more of his blood from spilling out onto the unforgiving pavement. Roman placed the ring into her palm and closed her fingers around it as he recited the long ago words he'd penned in a low, wavering voice filled with pain.

"I don't know you, but I see your face in the clouds.

I've never met you, but your smile fills my soul.

Some hear words, I only hear you calling to me.

Time might separate us, but it can't deny the bond we share.

With dreams only of you, I close my eyes."

Roman coughed again, more blood oozing out of his mouth, but still his eyes never left hers, and the peppermint-scented wood smoke continued to swirl around them. His voice was barely a whisper now, but it was as if he was screaming the words at her. "I love you, Varinia Velt. Twenty-four, twenty-five, or seventy-two years old. I love you."

Rin opened her mouth to tell him she loved him too, but his eyes closed and she felt his entire body go lax under her.

"Nooooo!" she moaned, clutching her fist with the ring inside to her heart, even as she put more of her weight on her other hand on his chest.

"I've got him now, ma'am, please move back," a stern voice commanded from her left.

Rin looked up, hardly able to see through the tears in her eyes, and saw a man in a blue uniform shirt kneeling next to them. She quickly glanced around. The police were handcuffing the man who'd held them up and the medics were checking him over.

There were two other EMTs standing behind her and Roman, waiting for her to move so they could help him.

The EMT next to her gently pushed her hand away from Roman's chest and put his own over the hole as soon as hers cleared it. He started barking orders to the men behind her, but Rin didn't hear any of it. She stood and backed away, clutching the ring to her chest with both hands now, not taking her eyes from Roman's. The eerie mist continued to swirl around him, but the EMTs didn't even seem to notice.

The poem he'd recited to her might as well have come from the depths of her own soul.

*I don't know you, but I see your face in the clouds.*
*I've never met you, but your smile fills my soul.*
*Some hear words, I only hear you calling to me.*
*Time might separate us, but it can't deny the bond we share.*
*With dreams only of you, I close my eyes.*

It was exactly what had been happening in her dreams forever. She couldn't lose him. Not now. Not after just finding him.

Rin watched as the EMTs loaded Roman onto a stretcher and carried him to the back of an ambulance, the misty fog rolling right along with them. The doors shut behind them and the vehicle pulled away from the scene, taking the only man she'd ever love with it.

"Ma'am? I'm Sergeant Wright. I understand you were the other victim here? Is any of that blood yours?"

Rin looked down at herself. Her hands were covered in Roman's blood and it was smeared on her beautiful yellow sweater. She shook her head, but didn't say anything more, couldn't say anything more through a throat that was so closed off, it was a miracle she was still breathing.

"Good. I'm glad you weren't hurt. I need to get your statement. Can you tell me what happened tonight?"

What happened? Rin knew he wasn't talking about the miracle of finding her one true love. Knew he didn't care about how two souls had managed to find each other even though the odds were against them. The police officer didn't want to know about the fog or poems or rings. She sighed and took a deep breath.

She needed to get to Roman. And the only way to do that was to tell the officer what she knew. Then she could go to the hospital. All thoughts of her birthday party, sister, and mom were gone. Roman was the only thing that mattered.

Rin slid the bloody ring she'd been clutching onto her finger and closed her eyes for a moment at the jolt of energy she felt racing down her arm into her chest. Roman. She felt him with her even when he wasn't physically there.

She looked down. The poesy ring was still crimson. It gave her hope. Surely if Roman died, the ring would go back to being dark gray again.

Sometime between them sitting on the bench and now, Rin had realized that the ring *was* about her. Her and Roman. Not her mom. Not Tina. Maybe not even MacKenzie.

Somehow her ancestors, going back to the original owner of the ring, Theodosia, had meant for *her* to have the ring. She'd grown up the way she had, all to make her compatible with Roman. Oh, there were a lot of ways they were different, but the bottom line was that if she had been brought up as Tina had been, she never would've appealed to Roman, and vice versa. She would've lost out and the ring would've stayed dark.

Rin turned to the cop, wanting to get this over with. She needed to get to the hospital. "We were sitting on the bench talking…"

# Chapter Eight

R IN SAT IN a fake leather chair in the emergency waiting room at the best trauma center in the city. She'd washed her hands, but was still wearing her bloody sweater. Her mom had urged her to go home and change, but Rin wasn't about to leave the hospital.

The last two hours had been a whirlwind. She'd gone back to the ballroom to grab her purse and keys so she could get to Roman, but had run into her mom, who'd promptly freaked out, rightly so, at the sight of her daughter covered in blood.

Rin didn't think they would leave the party, but Cassia caught a glimpse of the ring on her daughter's finger. It was a brilliant scarlet that couldn't be missed.

Her mom grabbed hold of the ring and looked into Rin's eyes. "It's red."

She'd nodded.

"Tina?" Cassia asked, turning to her other daughter.

Tina had merely shaken her head, telling her mom

that it wasn't red because of any feeling she'd had with any of the men she'd met that night.

Without another word, Cassia and Tina had insisted on coming to the hospital with her.

Rin wasn't surprised her mom immediately figured out Roman was the man she'd been hoping to find for Tina her entire life. She was a woman who'd grown up hearing stories about instant loves through the ages, so hearing Rin say she loved a man she'd met for the first time that night wasn't even a blip on her weird-o-meter. It was almost as if she wasn't surprised at all, but Rin knew her mom's head had to be reeling, learning that it wasn't Tina who was the key to breaking the curse, but Rin.

They'd raced to the hospital, only to find out that Roman's family had already been called. None of the staff would talk to Rin, since she wasn't a relative. She had to wait until his family got there, and since they had to drive over from Pennsylvania, it would be a few hours.

Roman's brothers arrived first, surprisingly quickly considering where they'd had to travel from. Rin would've been able to point them out as being related to Roman in a heartbeat if she didn't already know they were going to be showing up. They were both tall and handsome with dark hair, just like their brother. They had the same noses and seriously looked alike enough to almost be triplets.

They burst through the doors like their Roman namesakes might have done when entering into battle. Mouths drawn into tight lines, worry furrowing their brows. Rin didn't move, feeling awkward for the first time. She didn't know these men, they didn't know her.

Luckily, Cassia didn't have any reservations.

She approached the two men, introducing herself as the mother of Roman's girlfriend, and telling them that anything they could find out from the hospital staff would be appreciated, since they wouldn't tell them anything because they weren't related to Roman. The two men were obviously stressed out and devastated after hearing their big brother had been shot, but after they'd glanced over to where Cassia indicated, and saw Rin, they merely nodded in agreement before heading to the counter to speak to the employee sitting there.

Rin knew she looked like hell, but she couldn't imagine leaving the hospital for even a moment to go home and change. She glanced down at the ring, which she'd been obsessively turning on her finger over and over. Still crimson. Thank God. It gave her the small spark of hope she needed to know that Roman was still alive.

After speaking with the nurse, Roman's brothers came over to the corner of the room where Rin and her family were waiting.

"You're with Roman?" one of them asked, holding out his hand.

"Yes. I'm Varinia. I'm guessing you're his youngest brother, Gus?"

He nodded. Pleasantries taken care of, he got down to business. "Can you tell us what happened? All we have are sketchy details."

Rin swallowed. The last thing she wanted to do was get into it all again, especially before knowing how Roman was. She wished she was meeting his brothers under different circumstances. "Of course. But first, please...can you tell me what you found out about Roman? They wouldn't talk to us."

"He's in surgery," the other man told them. "The nurse said the bullet went into the top of his lung and bounced around inside his chest cavity. Her words, not mine."

Rin swayed in her seat as the imagery his words evoked raced inside her head.

"Easy, Varinia," Max told her, obviously seeing the impact his words had on her. He knelt in front of her and put a hand on her shoulder to steady her. "You're as pale as the tiles on the floor. Take a deep breath."

Rin did as Roman's brother suggested, feeling the blackness at the sides of her eyes recede. "He's going to live though, right?" Her words were whispered to Max, a question, but more like a plea.

"He's going to live," Gus confirmed from above them in a voice of steel. "My big brother isn't a quitter."

Rin nodded. "He was protecting me. The guy was threatening to kill us both if we didn't give him all our money and valuables. When the guy wouldn't back off, and looked like he was about to shoot us, Roman rushed him."

It was as if Gus expected her words. "I figured as much."

Max held out a hand. "It's good to meet you, Varinia."

She shook his hand solemnly. "Where are your kids? And wives?"

"They're on their way. We chartered a plane to get here as soon as we could. It only had two seats, so we grabbed 'em. Our parents, and the others, will be here as soon as they can. They're driving out."

Rin nodded, relieved that she didn't have to meet the whole Reese clan right this second. As kind and patient as his brothers were being, this wasn't the way she really wanted to meet his family. "This is my mom, Cassia, and sister, Tina," she told Max and Gus, gesturing to them.

They all nodded at each other.

Gus pulled a chair over from nearby and Max did the same. They sat huddled in the corner of the room, chatting somewhat awkwardly, getting to know each other.

"Augustina?" Gus asked.

"Augustus?" Tina returned with a smile.

Cassia smirked and commented, "I see I'm not the only one enthralled with Roman history."

Everyone chuckled, glad the tension in the air had been broken, at least for the moment.

It wasn't until Gus said, "That's a beautiful ring, is it an heirloom?" that Rin realized she hadn't talked about it with her mom or sister. They'd seen it in the ballroom when she'd shown up, bloody and freaked out and needing a ride to the hospital, but hadn't discussed it further.

"It's still red, Mom," Rin said in a soft voice, holding out her hand so her relatives could see it up close.

"I can't believe it," Tina said, turning her sister's hand right and left so the brilliant crimson sparkled in the fluorescent lights of the waiting room.

"I take it that's unusual?" Max asked, confused at the reactions of the women.

"It's a miracle," Cassia breathed.

For the first time in a long time, Rin saw her mom cry. She threw herself into Cassia's arms and felt Tina's arms wrap around them as well. The three of them sniffled for a bit before Rin finally pulled back and turned to Max and Gus with an explanation. She sat between them and held out her hand so they could clearly see the ring on her finger.

"The legend of the ring states, in a nutshell, that if the daughter doesn't find true love before she turns twenty-five, then she'll be doomed to a life of loneliness. No one in my family has found the man meant to be hers in decades. This is the first time we've ever known the ring to be anything but gray."

"Roman," Gus stated. It wasn't a question.

"Roman," Rin agreed with a small smile.

Gus put a hand on Rin's knee, and Max put his on the other. "Welcome to the family, Varinia. I have a feeling there's an interesting story behind your relationship with my brother, but I couldn't be happier he's finally found the princess he's been looking for all his life."

Rin smiled at Gus and tried not to cry. She thought Roman's family might balk at their quick courtship—hell, quick was an understatement. But it looked like she just might be welcomed after all.

"Family of Roman Reese," a no-nonsense voice said from the doorway.

They all turned to see a doctor, still in surgical scrubs, standing at the other end of the room. Gus and Max stood—but all Rin could do was stare at the surgeon.

A mist was hovering around his legs.

As soon as Rin looked at him, it slowly disentangled

itself from the man she had no doubt had saved Roman's life, and rolled across the floor.

As Rin watched, wide-eyed, it made its way over to her and enveloped her, wrapping the now-familiar scent of smoke, peppermint and a crisp fall day around her. She inhaled deeply, bringing it into her lungs and her very being.

"Come on, Rin, you're a part of this family now, let's go see what the doctor has to say about Roman."

Rin took hold of the hand Max held out to her and headed across the room toward her future. She had no doubt whatsoever that the doctor had good news for them. The misty fog, and the bright crimson ring on her finger, told her everything she needed to know.

# Chapter Nine

RIN SNUGGLED INTO Roman's side a couple of months later. She'd moved to Pennsylvania as soon as Roman had been released from the hospital, not willing to spend even one night away from him if she could help it. Her twenty-fifth birthday had come and gone without any fanfare, which was more than okay with Rin. She'd found her true love; it was the best present she ever could've received.

They were huddled on the huge brown suede couch in his living room. The doctor had told them that it had been touch and go for a while in the operating room, but he'd managed to stop the bleeding from Roman's kidney, which had been nicked by a bullet fragment. He'd patched up his lung and fixed other small tears as well.

It hadn't been hard for her to make the decision to quit her job in Columbus and move to Pennsylvania to be with Roman. She'd interviewed for several jobs and had managed to find a position with a bigger company, with more money and more benefits. She was thrilled with how everything seemed to be falling into place. Including her relationship with Roman.

The man who'd held them up was in jail. He'd had a warrant out for first-degree murder before his robbery attempt. Apparently, he'd killed his pregnant girlfriend and both his parents before fleeing to the streets to try to get enough money to head to Mexico. The attempted murder of Roman was almost small potatoes compared to the other charges he was facing, but they would both testify if and when it came time, to make sure he never saw the light of day again.

The entire situation was unbelievable, but Roman was alive and safe. Rin couldn't ask for any other outcome.

"Happy birthday, Varinia," Roman said in a soft voice.

"Thanks. Although you *do* realize you're about a month late, right?"

He chuckled. "Yeah, but I wasn't really able to help you celebrate on the actual day."

"True. But you know what?" Rin sat up in the circle of his arms so she could look him in the eye. "I got the best present this year. I don't need anything else, ever."

"Did the ring get back to England all right?"

Rin nodded. "Yeah, I heard from MacKenzie yesterday. The courier arrived with it right on time."

"You tell her we'll be out to see her sometime next year?"

"Of course. She was excited. Oh, and she sends her and James' prayers that you'll continue to heal without any problems."

"I told you I'm fine," Roman protested. "Even the doctor was impressed with how fast I'm healing."

"I know, I know, but I still worry about you."

Roman hugged Rin to his chest, tucking her head in the crook of his shoulder. Her favorite place to be.

"I love you, Varinia. And I have to say, no matter how many pictures we take in our life, that one," he gestured to the eleven-by-fourteen print that sat in a heavy silver frame on the bookcase across from them, "will always be my favorite."

Rin didn't pick up her head, but moved it just enough so that she could see the picture he'd gestured to. It was taken the day Roman was discharged from the hospital. They were standing next to each other in front of the automatic doors and Rin had one arm around Roman's back and the other resting on his chest, over his healing wound. One of his arms was around her shoulders and the other was holding her hand to his chest. The sun was hitting them just right and the poesy ring shone bright crimson in the sunlight. They weren't looking at the camera, but instead at each other. Rin could almost physically see the love between them.

"Agreed."

"Are you sad you had to send the ring back to Mac-Kenzie?" Roman asked, not for the first time.

"No," Rin said immediately. "It feels right. It's where it needs to be. That picture is all the reminder I need. I have you right here with me. It's enough."

"It's too bad about the smear in the picture though," Roman said after a moment.

Rin lifted her head in shock and looked at him. "You can see that?"

The first time Tina had shown her the picture, she'd seen the mist intertwined around her and Roman's legs. She'd mentioned it to her sister, but Tina apparently didn't see it. Just as none of the people that night, none of the hospital staff, and neither of Roman's brothers had seen the mist when it had enveloped Roman and the doctor. She just assumed that she was the only one who was able to see the light fog.

"Well, yeah," Roman said in disbelief. "It's hard to miss."

"Remind me to tell you the story sometime of how that smear relates to that awful night," Rin told him, snuggling back into him.

"I will. Have you heard from Tina?"

Rin smiled. "Yeah. She called from Vegas."

"I seriously can't believe she eloped with Luke."

"I know, right? She'd apparently been seeing him behind my mom's back for months. Given how my mom acted, Tina always thought Mom wanted her to be with someone rich, when all Mom *really* cared about was her finding her one true love. The fact that Luke was a roofer didn't faze her at all."

"Can't blame Tina for assuming," Roman mused. "I have to say, I like your sister a lot more now that she doesn't have 'desperate' tattooed on her forehead."

Rin knew she should be offended on behalf of her sister, but she agreed with Roman. She simply said, "Me too."

"There's something I've been wondering about, though," Roman said, lightly running his hand up and down Rin's back as he spoke.

"What's that?"

"If you only got the ring a few weeks or so before your birthday, how would Tina or your mom have known if she'd found her true love without it? I mean, she didn't have the ring growing up, so she couldn't be alerted by it changing color if she'd met 'the one' years ago, right?"

Rin shrugged. "I'm not sure. But I knew *you* were the man meant for *me* after only being in your presence for a few minutes. Maybe it didn't matter if I had the ring on or not. Maybe it *was* the reason I recognized your scent in the first place. We'll never know."

"I'd like to think it was fated, but Rin, it scares me to death to think of how close we came to never meeting."

Rin snuggled as close as she could to Roman and breathed his scent deep into her lungs, reassuring herself before she admitted softly, "Me too."

Sensing she needed a change in subject, Roman asked, "And your mom is dating now too?"

"She's seeing a realtor."

Roman chuckled, then sobered. "Have you talked to her about the legend at all?"

"A little," Rin told him. "She swears that she told the nurses when we were born to mark the oldest and they reported that they had. Who knows if they put the right identification band on the right baby." She shrugged. "But you know what? I don't care anymore. I love my mom and Tina. She wasn't the best parent, but I get that she did what she did out of desperation. Maybe we were a glitch in the cosmic blip of the world. Maybe the ring being reconnected with the sword disrupted something in the cosmos and allowed all three of us to find the men we were meant to be with. I'm just so in love with you that I couldn't really care."

Roman pushed Rin until she lay flat on her back on the couch. He leaned down and Rin smelled the peppermint he'd eaten earlier. She'd never get sick of his scent. Ever. She closed her eyes as his mouth brushed her earlobe, then the sensitive skin beneath it.

"The doctor cleared me today for physical activity," Roman whispered against her skin as he nipped and sucked at her.

"Ummmmm." Rin's mind had gone blank. All thoughts of legends and her mom and sister gone as if in a puff of smoke. All she could think about was how good Roman smelled and about how she wanted his lips to keep going down her body.

"I can't wait until next weekend to make you my wife."

His words reminded Rin of the question she'd wanted to ask him. "Your family doesn't think it's weird that we're getting married so quickly?"

"No, Varinia. They love you. They love you for *me*. Gus asked me a week after I was out of the hospital if I'd asked you to marry me yet. When I told him I was waiting for just the right moment, he smacked me on the head and told me to get on with it."

"Your niece and nephews are cute."

"Ummmmm." It was Roman's turn to ignore her statement. His hand moved up from her waist under her shirt and closed over her naked breast. "I had thought to wait until we were man and wife before making you mine in every way, but I don't think I can wait another day, let alone seven." He lifted his head and rested on his elbow on the cushion next to her. He brushed his thumb over her cheek and held her head still. "Will you let me love you?"

"For as long as you'll have me, every night if possible."

No more words were spoken between them as Roman's head dropped and his lips covered Rin's.

Every time they kissed, Rin felt as if she had come home. His tongue tangled with hers as his hand caressed her nipple, teasing it until it was as hard as a rock under his fingers.

"Lift your arms," he murmured against her lips.

She did, and the moment her shirt cleared her head, Roman had claimed her mouth again. After several moments, he nipped her lower lip and moved down her body, taking her bra straps over her shoulders as he went.

Rin looked down at the man she loved more than she could've ever imagined loving anyone as he concentrated on unhooking her bra. The look in his eyes when she lay under him topless was one she'd never get tired of. He'd seen her before, but it was as if each time was the first for him. His large hands covered her and he squeezed and plumped her breasts.

"I will never take you for granted, Rin," he swore, looking up into her eyes as his hands continued to caress her. "I love you. I can't wait to make you mine."

"I'm already yours," Rin breathed as he lowered his

head and took one of her nipples into his mouth. She shifted under him, bending her knees and squeezing his torso tightly as he worshiped her body.

"Please, Roman. I want you," Rin begged.

At her words, he pushed her legs flat on the couch and stood up, holding out his hand. Rin didn't hesitate and allowed Roman to help her stand.

Without a word, he led the way down the hall to his bedroom. They'd slept together every night in his bed, but Rin's heart beat fast in her chest, knowing neither of them would sleep for a very long time tonight.

It was much, much later when they lay exhausted and replete in their large bed, legs tangled together, sweat drying on their sated bodies, that Rin said the words she'd repeated in her head over and over since the night they'd been attacked.

"I don't know you, but I see your face in the clouds.

I've never met you, but your smile fills my soul.

Some hear words, I only hear you calling to me.

Time might separate us, but it can't deny the bond we share.

With dreams only of you, I close my eyes."

Roman sighed and tightened his hold on her as she continued. "I want those words to be our wedding vows. I've never heard anything so beautiful in all my life."

"Done," Roman agreed immediately. "Close your eyes, dream only of me, as I will of you."

Rin snuggled into her love, smiling as her Guardian Mist settled over the two of them. She fell asleep, secure in the knowledge that the fates had finally smiled on her family and delivered her man to her.

HOURS LATER, IN the darkest part of the night, when humans and animals alike are in the deepest sleep, the mist surrounding the couple on the bed swirled around them as Rin dreamed.

She dreamed of a large banquet hall, filled with people wearing costumes from across the ages. It looked like a costume party, except Rin somehow knew the clothes the men and women wore were authentic. There were men in Scottish kilts with brightly colored plaids thrown over their shoulders, huge puffy Regency dresses, togas, powdered hair, corsets, and enough weaponry strapped to the men to make even the most liberal twentieth-century man nervous.

It was a party like none Rin had ever seen. She walked into the room and the people parted in front of her, as if they'd been waiting for her to arrive. Rin looked down, nervous about what was happening, and smiled as she saw the mist around her feet, following along with her. Relieved, she looked up—and saw Roman standing halfway down the makeshift aisle that had formed by the spectators at the banquet hall.

He was standing in a tuxedo, holding a hand out to her. She got closer and smiled when she saw the bow tie he was wearing was camouflage. Leave it to him to put a bit of himself in the formal attire.

"We've been waiting for you, Varinia." He spoke in a quiet voice, but one which was full of love. He kissed the back of her hand and tucked it into the crook of his arm as they turned to face the front of the room.

Rin felt the warmth of Roman against her side and was surprised to realize she was now wearing a dark emerald-green dress. It was sleeveless and floor length. The bodice was covered in hundreds of sequins, making it sparkle in the light from the chandeliers overhead. It had a small train, so as they walked forward she felt it flow out behind her gracefully. She felt like a princess. Roman's fairytale princess.

Looking over to her left, Rin saw her sister and mother. Tina was waving madly and her mom gave her a small smile. Luke was standing next to Tina and there was a man standing behind her mom, but Rin couldn't make out his face.

Roman nudged her and pointed off to his right with his head. Rin looked and saw her half-sister standing next to her husband. They looked regal and extremely happy. Rin smiled up at Roman.

They came to a halt in front of a group of about a dozen people. The women all had varying shades of red hair, and were dressed in what looked like costumes from different times in history. Their men were all tall and brawny. It dawned on Rin, suddenly, what she was seeing.

These were some of her relatives. Valeria, Antonia, Valeriana, Annie, and Britannia. The women who'd found their true loves, just as she had. She knew without a doubt that they'd had the same fears and worries she'd felt before they'd found their loves. Rin looked each woman in the eye and smiled shyly. Yeah, they knew.

A woman dressed in a long white robe stepped forward, a handsome man in a toga by her side.

"Welcome, Varinia. I have waited a long time to meet you. I am Theodosia. We have been watching you and your family, and are happy to have you join us. The road to love is never an easy one, as any of us could tell you." She gestured to the women standing near her, then continued.

"Thank you for taking care of The Lucius Ring. Go and live your life. Be happy. You will be blessed with many children, and your daughter, and her daughter, and all the daughters to come, will find their true loves without the worry of the legend hanging over their heads. The ring has come to rest where it belongs, with The Theodosia Sword. Thank you for bringing the ring full circle and being open to finding your true love."

Rin opened her mouth to say something, though she

wasn't sure what, when the mist at her feet rose up and obscured her vision from everyone in the room. It was as if they were suddenly caught in a thick fog bank. Rin turned into Roman and clutched him tightly, sighing in relief when she felt his arms band around her. One of his hands settled on her lower back and the other between her shoulder blades. She inhaled, knowing she'd never get enough of his peppermint, smoky scent.

It could've been hours or minutes, but the next thing Rin knew, she was stirring in Roman's bed, her nose buried in the space between his neck and shoulder. One leg was thrown over his and one of Roman's hands was resting on her hip.

Rin smiled, loving that her ancestors had visited her in her dream, and that she would never have to worry about her own daughter having to go through the same angst her family had for generations.

Dreams only of you. How true the legend was.

"Sleep well?" Roman asked in a gruff voice, obviously still half asleep himself.

"Yeah. I love you."

"Love you too. I'm not ready to get up yet…ten more minutes?"

Ten more minutes of snuggling up to her man without a care in the world? Absolutely.

"Ten more minutes, Roman."

Rin put her head back down and inhaled deeply,

contentment spreading throughout her body. She had a million things to do. Work. Finish planning a wedding. Call her sister. Arrange a trip to England to meet MacKenzie...the list went on and on. But here in Roman's arms, time ceased to pass. It was just her and the love of her life. Everything else could wait.

**To sign up for Susan's Newsletter go to:**
http://bit.ly/SusanStokerNewsletter

**Or text:** STOKER to 24587 for text alerts on your mobile device

# Discover other titles by Susan Stoker

## Badge of Honor: Texas Heroes Series
*Justice for Mackenzie*

*Justice for Mickie*

*Justice for Corrie*

*Justice for Laine (novella)*

*Shelter for Elizabeth*

*Justice for Boone*

*Shelter for Adeline (Jan 2017)*

*Shelter for Sophie (Aug 2017)*

*Justice for Sidney (Oct 2017)*

*Shelter for Blythe (TBA)*

*Justice for Milena (TBA)*

*Justice for Kinley (TBA)*

*Shelter for Promise (TBA)*

*Shelter for Koren (TBA)*

*Shelter for Penelope (TBA)*

## Unsung Heroes: Delta Force
*Rescuing Rayne*

*Assisting Aimee – Loosely related to DF*

*Rescuing Emily*

*Rescuing Harley (Nov 2016)*

*Marrying Emily (Spring 2017)*

*Rescuing Kassie (May 2017)*

*Rescuing Bryn (Nov 2017)*

*Rescuing Casey (TBA)*

*Rescuing Wendy (TBA)*
*Rescuing Mary (TBA)*

**Ace Security Series**
*Claiming Grace (Mar 2017)*
*Claiming Alexis (July 2017)*
*Claiming Bailey (TBA)*

**SEAL of Protection Series**
*Protecting Caroline*
*Protecting Alabama*
*Protecting Alabama's Kids*
*Protecting Fiona*
*Marrying Caroline (novella)*
*Protecting Summer*
*Protecting Cheyenne*
*Protecting Jessyka*
*Protecting Julie (novella)*
*Protecting Melody*
*Protecting the Future*

**Stand Alone:**
*The Guardian Mist*

**Beyond Reality Series**
*Outback Hearts*
*Flaming Hearts*
*Frozen Hearts*

**Writing as Annie George**
*Stepbrother Virgin (erotic novella)*

# Connect with Susan Online

### Susan's Facebook Profile and Page:
www.facebook.com/authorsstoker
www.facebook.com/authorsusanstoker

### Follow Susan on Twitter:
www.twitter.com/Susan_Stoker

### Find Susan's Books on Goodreads:
www.goodreads.com/SusanStoker

### Email: Susan@StokerAces.com

### Website: www.StokerAces.com

### To sign up for Susan's Newsletter go to:
http://bit.ly/SusanStokerNewsletter

### Or text: STOKER to 24587 for text alerts on your mobile device

# About the Author

*New York Times, USA Today,* and *Wall Street Journal* Bestselling Author Susan Stoker has a heart as big as the state of Texas, where she lives, but this all-American girl has also spent the last fourteen years living in Missouri, California, Colorado, and Indiana. She's married to a retired Army man who now gets to follow *her* around the country.

She debuted her first series in 2014 and quickly followed that up with the SEAL of Protection Series, which solidified her love of writing and creating stories readers can get lost in.

If you enjoyed this book, or any book, please consider leaving a review. It's appreciated by authors more than you'll know.

CPSIA information can be obtained
at www.ICGtesting.com
Printed in the USA
LVOW13s1021270617
539531LV00018B/295/P